OTHER YEARLING BOOKS YOU WILL ENJOY:

ALL-OF-A-KIND-FAMILY, *Sydney Taylor*
ELLA OF ALL-OF-A-KIND-FAMILY, *Sydney Taylor*
BALLET SHOES, *Noel Streatfeild*
DANCING SHOES, *Noel Streatfeild*
FAMILY SHOES, *Noel Streatfeild*
MOVIE SHOES, *Noel Streatfeild*
NEW SHOES, *Noel Streatfeild*
SKATING SHOES, *Noel Streatfeild*
TENNIS SHOES, *Noel Streatfeild*
THEATRE SHOES, *Noel Streatfeild*

YEARLING BOOKS are designed especially to entertain and enlighten young people. Charles F. Reasoner, Professor Emeritus of Children's Literature and Reading, New York University, is consultant to this series.

For a complete listing of all Yearling titles, write to Dell Publishing Co., Inc., Promotion Department, P.O. Box 3000, Pine Brook, N.J. 07058.

SYDNEY TAYLOR

All-Of-A-Kind
Family
Downtown

Illustrations by Beth and Joe Krush

A YEARLING BOOK

Published by
DELL PUBLISHING CO., INC.
1 Dag Hammarskjold Plaza
New York, New York 10017
Text copyright © 1972 by Sydney Taylor
Illustrations copyright © 1972 by Follett Publishing Company, a
division of Follett Corporation
All rights reserved.
No portion of this book may be reproduced
in any form without written permission from
Follett Publishing Company.
For information address
Follett Publishing Company, Chicago, Illinois 60607.
Yearling ® TM 913705, Dell Publishing Co., Inc.
ISBN: 0-440-42032-6
Reprinted by arrangement with Follett Publishing Company
Printed in the United States of America

October 1973

10 9 8 7

MPC

To Tanta—always there when needed

Charlotte Catches
1: the Stove

CHARLOTTE NUDGED her little sister. "Wake up, Gertie! I catched the stove this morning!"

Henny bounced out of bed. "That's not fair!" she cried, her tousled blond curls swinging back and forth angrily. "You had it yesterday!"

"I know I did," answered Charlotte. "But last night, remember, right after supper, I said 'I catch the stove tomorrow morning,' before anyone else did. And you heard me with your very own ears!"

Big sister Ella yawned sleepily. "That's right. She said it first. That's the rule. Whoever says it first."

Gertie, now thoroughly awake, stuck her tongue out at Henny. "See!"

Henny snuggled back hurriedly under her warm featherbed. "This bedroom is just like an icebox!" she grumbled.

Sarah lay curled up like a small kitten against Ella's warm body. Only her pale, blond braids stuck out above the coverlet. Ella couldn't resist giving the braids a gentle tweak. "You up, Sarah?" she asked softly.

"Umm . . . mmm," Sarah mumbled.

Their school clothes lay neatly arranged on the three

chairs alongside their beds. The girls always laid them out the night before. Mama said it saved lots of time in the morning.

Suddenly, the two smallest nightgowned figures sprang out of bed and gathered up their clothes. Gertie was close behind Charlotte as they sped across the cold bare floor toward the warm kitchen.

"I guess we might as well get up, too," said Ella.

Henny groaned. "Wish I didn't have to go to school today. We're having a history test. Who can remember all those dates, anyway? If I could only get Mama to let me stay home and help her. After all," she added hopefully, "there's a lot of extra work with another baby around the house."

Don't even bother asking," Ella advised. "You know Mama would never let you get out of going to school."

"I guess not," Henny agreed dolefully.

Now the three older sisters hopped out of bed, whisked their clothes off the chairs, and joined the two others in the kitchen. "Good morning, Mama," they greeted in chorus.

"Morning, girls," Mama replied, as quietly and swiftly she went about getting breakfast ready.

It was good to be in the warm, cozy kitchen. On the big coal stove, cocoa was heating in one pot and oatmeal bubbled cheerily in another. A tray on a shelf above the stove was stacked temptingly with fresh, crusty rolls. Mama's morning coffee, coming slowly to a boil, added its own fragrance to the other delicious odors. The girls sniffed the air hungrily.

Sprawled in the rocker, Charlotte was already in possession of the "catched" spot, directly in front of the stove. Her stockinged feet were propped up on the shiny, nickel-plated ledge which jutted out to one side like a shelf. She wriggled her warm toes. On the floor beside her, Gertie sat struggling with a button hook in a valiant attempt to button her own shoes.

On such a cold November morning, the nearer you got to the stove, the warmer you felt. From their places on the brown leather couch, the older sisters looked enviously at Charlotte and Gertie. What a shame, they were thinking, that there was room for only two.

"Mama," wailed Gertie, "I can't hook in the button!"

"Come here to me," Ella said. "I'll help you." She turned to Mama. "The baby still sleeping?"

"Yes. He had his breakfast very early."

"When is he going to stop sleeping so much?" demanded Gertie. "I never get a chance to play with him."

"He's not even three months old, Gertie," Mama said. "He needs lots of sleep to make him grow. He'll be staying up more when he gets a little older. You wait and see. Now — who's ready for hair combing?"

Everyone was — that is, everyone except Charlotte. The girls lined up by size, with Ella first because she was Mama's helper. Mama brushed and combed out the tangles, and Ella did the prettying up. She tied on the bows, and she also twined Henny's curls around her finger till they hung like smooth, shiny bottles.

Meanwhile, the rocking chair was moving back and forth in a lazy singsong swing. Charlotte felt herself drifting along drowsily. How pleasant it was! Her eyes traveled to the iron poker hanging on the wall. What does it feel like when you use a poker, she wondered. It always seems to slide into the slot so smoothly when Mama raises the stove lid. She stood up and reached for the poker. It curved in a lovely graceful way, like the neck of a swan, yet it was heavy in her hand. Carefully she set it in place so that she could lift up one of the smooth round lids. The lid was much heavier than she had imagined. She had to hold on with both hands. Slowly she pushed the lid away toward the back of the stove and peered into the bed of glowing coals nestled snugly inside. They were so pretty — all orange and red — and had such odd shapes. Tiny blue flames were licking them gently. Shimmering waves of heat rose upward, swirling and twisting like a genie. Just like the genie that was hidden inside Aladdin's wonderful lamp! There was a genie living inside the stove, too. It was he who had rubbed those coals, making them glow. He had said, "Shine brightly, my jewels! Make this kitchen warm and comfortable." The jewels had obeyed.

Come to think of it, she had never looked into the grate when the stove was on. She got down on her knees, swung

out the cover, and gazed inside. The coals shifted a little. Some small sparkling pieces popped into the grate below. Toward morning, when the stove grew cold, Charlotte knew they would turn to ashes. Papa would shovel them out and throw them into the garbage pail. Charlotte sighed unhappily over the plight of the genie's jewels.

She pushed the poker around inside the grate, pulling some of the more interesting pieces toward her. Already, thin streaks of gray were slowly creeping along their edges. Oh, they were lovely! She sat back on her heels staring at them, fascinated. Her face grew hot; her eyes were beginning to smart. She'd have to move back a little. I could pull out some of the jewels and play with them on the floor, she told herself. Gently she pushed the blazing coals nearer and nearer with the poker, till finally they toppled over the edge — right into the skirt of her pinafore!

She held the pinafore away from her body and gazed downward, smiling happily. How brightly the pieces glistened against the white of her apron! They were beautiful, utterly beautiful!

All at once she noticed a stain of brown forming in the center of her apron. It spread itself slowly. Now a tiny flame appeared. Hungrily it began feeding on the cloth. Oh my, thought Charlotte in dismay, look at the hole in my apron! What will Mama say?

Hastily she spilled the coals out onto the floor. But she could not spill out the flame. It flared in an ever-widening circle. She bent forward and began to beat her apron against the floor. It was no use. She could not stamp it out. Now several tongues of flame caught hold of her dress. A stab of fear set her heart pounding. She wanted to call out for help, but her breath was coming in frightened gasps.

It all occurred so quickly, the family was unaware of what was happening. Mama was busily plaiting Sarah's hair when suddenly Henny let out a startled scream, "Mama, Charlotte's burning up!"

Sarah's pigtails sprang apart as the comb clattered to the floor. Swiftly Mama snatched up the rug lying in front of the couch, and flung it over Charlotte. She rolled her over and over on the kitchen floor, while the other girls watched in fear. Only Henny was racing back and forth alongside the whirling rug. "Should I go get Papa?" she shrieked.

"No! It's not necessary!" Mama shouted back. She unrolled the rug. There was no more fire. There was just a rumpled looking little girl who sat up, staring about her in bewilderment. Quickly, the sisters gathered around.

Gertie dropped to her knees beside her favorite sister. "Are you hurted, Charlotte?" she asked anxiously.

Charlotte swept the tumbled brown hair back from her forehead. Her eyes blinked uncertainly. "I smell burned," she said, wrinkling her nose in displeasure. "But I guess I'm all right."

Mama took a deep breath. It sounded like a big sigh. "Of course, she's all right," she assured them all.

"Oh, Charlotte! You scared the life out of us!" cried Ella.

"I'm still shaking," Sarah added.

But all Charlotte could think of was — would Mama scold her? After all, she was a big girl, seven years old already. She ought to know better than to play with burning coals. Her apron was ruined, and her dress had a great big hole right in front. It was her good woolen school dress, too. She looked up at Mama with worried eyes.

Mama didn't scold. She just held Charlotte close for a moment. "We were very lucky," she said. "Come. You'd better wash up. I'll get you a clean apron. It'll cover up the hole for now. I'll mend it this afternoon. But you'll have to wear a dress with a patch in it for the rest of the term, Charlotte. We can't afford a new dress."

Charlotte hung her head. She was close to tears. "I

know," she whispered. "I'm sorry, Mama. I didn't mean to . . ." It was hard to explain. "The coals . . . they looked pretty . . . and . . . and I thought they looked like . . . when I saw them in my apron . . . ."

"In your apron!" Ella exclaimed. "Whatever in the world made you put them there?"

"I didn't put them there." The tears were rolling down. "They just . . . fell . . . in."

"Never mind," Mama broke in, "I'm sure Charlotte's learned a lesson today." She helped her into a fresh pinafore.

Charlotte sniffed back her tears. Her hands smoothed the starched white pinafore. "See, Gertie, it covers up the hole." Then she added a bit more cheerfully. "Nobody'll ever know I got a patch in my dress because I always wear an apron anyway."

One Stop
After
2: Another

ALL WEEK LONG Mama's girls looked for-
ward to Friday — library day. Right after school, they hurried home to gather up the books they had borrowed the
week before.

"Ella," Mama said, "on the way, I want you to stop off
at the shop and give Papa this sandwich. It's the second time
this week he hasn't come home for lunch. It's a busy time
for him."

"All right, Ma."

"Come on!" Henny urged. "Let's not be too late. All
the best books will be gone."

Papa's junk shop was not far from where they lived.
Soon the five girls were cautiously making their way down

the steep, narrow staircase which led into the shop. "Kerchoo!" went Gertie as her little nose was tickled by the familiar dank, basement smell.

Just as they reached the bottom step, the shop door flew open and a young boy came dashing out. Wham! Henny suddenly found herself sprawled on the basement steps, staring into a pair of astonished black eyes.

"Hey!" Henny cried angrily as soon as she had recovered her breath. "Why don't you watch where you're going?"

The boy didn't answer; he just stood there uncertainly. Five pair of inquisitive eyes studied the stranger. He was thin, with a rather pale face. He was wearing a faded blue sweater over a much mended pair of short pants. His ragged cap had bounced off his head revealing a shock of thick curly hair. He tried to scoot around Henny, but the way was blocked by her sisters.

"I want to get by," he said, and began to push forward.

"Just a minute!" snapped Henny. "And stop pushing! We have to come down first. It's too narrow."

The boy stepped back, allowing the girls to pass. "Sorry," he mumbled as he started up the stairs.

"You forgot your cap!" Henny yelled after him.

The boy's thin legs came to a sudden halt.

"What's your name?" Henny asked in a more friendly tone.

No reply.

"You live around here?"

A quick nod of the head.

"Then you must go to our school. What grade are you in? I bet I'm older than you."

The boy grabbed his cap, flew up the stairs, and disappeared from sight.

"Well! How do you like that!" exclaimed Henny. "He ran off so fast—like we were poison or something!"

"So unfriendly," Sarah commented.

"Maybe he's shy," said Charlotte.

The children clustered around Papa's desk. "Who is that boy, Papa?" Henny asked.

"He's a little Italian boy. His name is Guido. Lately, he's been coming in with old newspapers, rags, and bottles. He earns himself a little money that way."

"Papa, it's freezing outside and all he has on is a torn sweater!" Ella exclaimed. "Does he always go around like that?"

"Yes," Papa replied. "I guess his folks must be very poor. Once I offered him a good coat instead of money but he wouldn't take it. So I try to keep him down here a little

21

while to give him a chance to warm up by the stove. But he always seems to be in such a hurry."

"He certainly was today!" declared Henny. "He —"

"Papa," Ella interrupted, "here's a sandwich Mama made for you. We have to hurry too. We're on our way to the library."

Out on the street, Gertie tugged at Ella's arm. "Couldn't we go to the settlement house instead?"

"The settlement house? What for?"

"They have a library."

"But we already belong to the public library."

"Not me. They won't let me. You have to be in 1B first and I'm only in 1A. But in the settlement house you can get a book even when you aren't old enough to belong to the regular library. A girl in my class told me."

"By next term, you'll be able to get a card from our library," Sarah consoled.

"But that's too long to wait," insisted Gertie.

"I always read to you from my library book," Charlotte said.

"But it's still not the same as having your own book. Please, please Ella, I want to have my own book."

"It's a long walk."

"You always walk there for the chorus, and Henny for her dancing class. If you can walk there, so can I."

But we have to return our books," Charlotte reminded.

Sarah looked at Gertie's pleading face. "Oh, let's do it. We can just hand in our books and get some new ones quickly. We don't have to stay around as long as we usually do."

"All right," agreed Ella.

"Some library day this is," remarked Henny. "One stop after another." She caught hold of Gertie's hand. "C'mon, let's run."

Never had the girls made their book selections so rapidly. In no time at all they were on their way to the settlement house.

As they crossed the street, Henny pointed to a tall, robust figure just ahead of them. "Ella, look! Isn't that Miss Carey?"

Ella noted the straight back, the lifted head. Of course. That couldn't be anybody but Miss Carey. That was the way she always walked, erect and sure, her feet setting down firmly on the pavement as if they knew exactly where they were going and why. "It is Miss Carey," she answered.

"Who's she?" Gertie asked Charlotte.

Charlotte shrugged. "I don't know. Maybe she's a nurse. She's got a black bag like the nurses carry."

"She is a nurse," Ella informed them. "From the settlement house. The long coat she's wearing covers up her uniform. That's why you couldn't tell. She's very nice."

"Come on. Let's catch up with her. Miss Carey!" yelled Henny. "Miss Carey!"

Miss Carey wheeled about. "Hello, Henny. Ella, too. How nice to see you!" Her voice was low-pitched, clear and pleasant.

"We're on our way to the settlement house," Henny declared.

"So am I," Miss Carey said. "Shall we go together?"

"Oh, yes," Ella replied at once.

From beneath the broad brim of her hat, Miss Carey's dark eyes swept over the five little bundled-up figures. "Is this the rest of the family?" she asked.

"Yes," answered Ella. "This is Sarah. She's the middle sister. Next comes Charlotte . . ."

"And do you know what Charlotte went and did the other day?" Henny put in. "She started a fire! Right in our own house! You should have seen it! Great, big, whopping flames shooting up all around her!"

"Oh, my!" cried Miss Carey. "Anyone hurt?"

"No. No one," Ella said reassuringly. "Henny's just making it out worse than it really was. Of course if it hadn't been for Mama . . ."

"Mama was wonderful!" Sarah broke in, her pale face lighting up. "She was so brave!"

"We all could have been burned alive!" Henny shouted dramatically.

"Oh, Henny, stop exaggerating!" cried Ella.

"Well, we could have!" Henny insisted.

"Suppose we let Ella tell all about it," suggested Miss Carey.

So Ella told the whole story and when she had finished, Miss Carey said, "Well, I'm certainly glad it turned out the way it did! Your Mama did exactly the right thing. You see, the rug cut off the air and smothered the flames."

"Can you imagine anyone putting hot coals in her apron?" Henny tapped herself on the head. "No brains!"

Charlotte shut her lips tight. She wouldn't even bother to answer. Henny knew perfectly well she hadn't put the coals in her apron on purpose. They just fell there . . . .

Miss Carey stole a glance at Charlotte. She slipped her arm around her and smiled. "Burning coals look very beautiful, don't they?"

Gratefully, Charlotte turned her face up to Miss Carey.

26

She wondered that this strange lady could understand so well. Her gaze traveled across the nurse's face. She's an older lady, like Mama. She's got such nice big eyes. Her nose is straight and it's just right — not too big and not too small. When her mouth is closed, she looks strict. But not when she smiles, I bet she's a wonderful nurse. If I had gotten burned, then Mama would let her come and be my nurse — and —

"Do you like being a nurse?" asked Sarah.

"Yes, very much," Miss Carey replied.

"Is it hard work?"

Miss Carey smiled. "Sometimes."

"Do you live around here?" Charlotte asked.

"Yes," Miss Carey replied. "In the settlement house with the other nurses. That makes it easy to find us whenever we are needed."

"Miss Carey, why don't you work uptown with the rich people, instead of down here on the East Side?" Henny asked. "Then you could make lots of money."

Miss Carey gave a little chuckle. "But I like this section of New York, and I like the people here." She turned to Gertie. "Which little sister are you?"

"I'm Gertie."

"And how old are you, Gertie?"

"Five. Almost five and a half."

"Last year we were all even. But this year we're all odd," Sarah chimed in.

"You mean because the year 1913 is an odd number?"

"Well, that too," Sarah replied. "But what I really mean is that this year Gertie's five years old. Charlotte's seven. I'm nine. Henny's eleven, and Ella's thirteen. All odd numbers. And even our baby brother Charlie is three months old. That's odd, too. See?"

Miss Carey nodded gravely. "I see."

By this time, they had reached the settlement. Miss Carey opened the door. "It's nice to have you visiting our settlement all in a bunch. Is there anything special going on this afternoon?"

"We came to get a book for me," Gertie announced firmly.

"You've come on the right day. On Friday our library is turned over to the littlest readers like you."

"There! What did I tell you!" a triumphant Gertie said. "Now I can take out my own book."

"Oh, I'm sorry. Ours is not a lending library. The books are not allowed out. It's really just a quiet place where you can sit and read."

"You mean I can't take the book home?"

"No. But you can stay as long as you like and read it here."

You could see Gertie's mouth droop at the corners. Her eyes squeezed shut. The sisters looked at one another. Was she going to cry?

"Gertie," Ella said quickly, "let's all go out to the backyard. You can sit in the glider swing."

Without a word, Gertie turned and started toward the door.

"Wait, Gertie," Miss Carey spoke up. "I just remembered. I have some children's books of my own." She hesitated a moment. They belonged to someone a long time ago. "They're in my room. Come along and pick one out for yourself."

Gertie smiled and slipped her hand into Miss Carey's. Together they climbed up the stairs.

She was down shortly. "Look! I got a book. It's *Reynard the Fox!*" she cried. "And I don't have to give it back, either. It's mine for keeps. Miss Carey said so."

"Ooh, lucky you!" Charlotte exclaimed. "Only why didn't you pick out one that's not so hard? You'll never be able to read it by yourself."

"I don't care. It's got lots of pictures. Miss Carey said

I could look at the pictures. And then you can read me the story, Charlotte," she added.

As she skipped ahead of her sisters, Gertie kept singsonging over and over, "I have a book of my own! I have a book of my own!"

3: *Christmas Stockings*

HENNY WENT SKIPPING down the windy
street on her way to her friend Fanny's house. Just think!
Today the Christians are starting their big holiday. No
school for more than a week! Isn't it great! Henny almost
laughed aloud. She and Fanny would have to make lots of
plans.

We could go to the movies. In the daytime, the two of
us can get in for only five cents. Let's see. If I could only
manage to save my daily allowance for just two days, I'd
have two pennies and Fanny, I'm sure, would be willing to
chip in the other three.

Maybe I ought to tell Fanny we should stop first at her
Papa's beer saloon. The last time her Papa took a whole

nickle from his cash register and tossed it to us. "Go on, kids. Enjoy yourselves!" Well, maybe if we're lucky, it might happen again today.

"Oops!" She'd never even noticed Mary Sullivan coming toward her.

"Hey, watch out!" Mary cried in alarm. She was clutching a big, beautiful doll close to her.

"Mary Sullivan," gasped Henny, "where on earth did you ever get that?"

Mary hugged the doll even closer, her face a picture of pure bliss. "Isn't she beautiful?"

Henny recovered quickly. "Well, I wouldn't know," she replied airily. "I'm much too grown-up for dolls." Nevertheless, she couldn't hide her delight in the doll's lovely outfit. It was a pink frock with little blue rosettes embroidered on it, with starched lace petticoats peeking out from underneath. Even the dainty white kid shoes were adorable.

"Is it a Christmas present?" she inquired.

"Uh huh. From our church."

Henny was incredulous. "You mean you get a present like that from your church at Christmas time?"

"Uh huh. They always give out presents for the holiday. People get baskets of food and clothes, and there's always toys for the children. And you don't have to belong to get something, either. They give it to anybody, so long as they need it."

Henny regarded the doll thoughtfully. Wheels in her head began turning. Just imagine if Charlotte or Gertie owned such a doll like that! Would they be thrilled! "The people at your church are very kind, aren't they?" she commented.

Mary beamed. "They really are. Especially at Christmas."

"Well, so long, Mary," Henny said with an abrupt wave of her hand. "I've got something important to do. I'm sure glad you got such a gorgeous doll."

Mary Sullivan really is poor, Henny said to herself, as she walked away. Everybody knows how hard up her family is. Those hand-me-down clothes she wears are always either too big or too small. And her busted-up shoes. Her folks don't even have enough money to buy her a decent hair ribbon. No wonder those church people gave her the doll.

By this time, all memory of Fanny — the movies — had slithered out of Henny's head. Instead, she found herself scurrying back toward home and right into Mr. Basch's grocery store.

"Mr. Basch," she cried breathlessly, "can you lend me a pair of scissors?"

Mr. Basch peered at her over his glasses. "Scissors? So what do you want with scissors?"

"I have to cut something in a hurry, and I can't find ours upstairs."

"So they're in the back room. I'll get them." He shuffled off and soon returned with a big pair of shears.

"Thanks." Shears in hand, Henny headed for the door.

"Hey, where are you going with my scissors?"

"Oh, I'll bring them back, don't worry."

Outside, she plopped down on the stoop of the house, shears poised over her outstretched legs. For one fleeting moment, she hesitated. But only for a moment.

Snip — snip! Through the knee of Mama's hand-knitted stocking the shears went. The stitches fell away. Snip — snip — snip again! A patch of white underwear showed through a big round hole.

Now for the other stocking. Down along the shinbone this time. Snip — snip !

The scissors hovered in midair. Dare she cut a hole in her coat, too? Nah! It won't be necessary. It's chinchilla cloth, but Papa had gotten it secondhand, and it looks shabby enough.

Back into Mr. Basch's store she went, walking sideways so he wouldn't notice the holes.

"Thanks, Mr. Basch," she said. She laid the shears on the counter and ran out.

A sudden thought overcame her. They've been giving things away all day. Maybe by now there wasn't anything left! She'd better rush right over!

She began to run, her golden curls bouncing against the

biting wind. She ran all the way. But when finally she arrived at her destination, she stopped short. It was a church! A real Christian church that she, a Jewish girl, was going into!

Warily her eyes traveled up the broad stone staircase. It was such a tremendous place! Much bigger than Papa's little synagogue. There was something awesome about it, too. Up and up went Henny's eyes, till at last she was staring up at the cross which rose majestically from the top of the building. She shivered, shutting her eyes tight against the sight. Would God be angry with her? Could she dare go inside a church? Or, even worse, ask for a present?

As she stood there, hesitating, she suddenly noticed a sign on the house next door. "Welcome neighbors. Come in and get your Christmas gifts!"

Oh! There was no need for her to go into the church after all. No need at all. She was safe. She raced up the steps of the little house.

Inside, a line of people were gathered before a long table piled high with all sorts of things. Henny was somewhat dismayed to find they were mostly grown-ups, with an occasional child holding tight to its parent's hand. Mary had made no mention about having to come with a parent. Would it matter, she wondered? Oh, dear! After all the trouble she'd gone to. Ruining her stockings and all. Maybe now she wouldn't be able to get a thing.

When finally it was her turn, the gray-haired lady sitting behind the table smiled warmly at her. "You here all alone?" she inquired.

Henny nodded.

"Couldn't mother come?"

"No. She . . . she's working."

That's not really a lie, Henny told herself immediately. Even though the lady probably thinks Mama's working in a factory or something. After all—Mama is working, what with six kids and the house and Papa and everything. She could feel the lady studying her. I hope she notices my stockings, she thought. To make sure, she bent down and began tugging at them.

There was a look of compassion on the lady's face. Emboldened, Henny blurted out, "My friend is Mary Sullivan. You gave her a beautiful doll!"

"Is that what you would like?" the lady asked.

"Uh huh."

"I'm not sure we have any left. Just a moment. I'll look in the other room."

Henny waited anxiously, shifting from one foot to the other. Soon the lady was back with a twin sister to Mary's doll in her arms. "You're lucky. This is the very last one."

Henny stuck the doll under her arm. "Oh, thank you," she mumbled. The next moment she was on her way to the door.

"Wait!" the lady called after her. "There's some food . . . perhaps your mother would . . . ."

"My mama will come another time," Henny called back hurriedly.

"I see. Good-bye then. And a merry Christmas to you."

Henny stopped at the door. "Happy Hanukah!" she returned boldly.

The lady's eyes opened wide. Her face broke into a broad smile. "Happy Hanukah!" she repeated.

Henny fairly danced along the sidewalk. It had all been so unbelievably easy. How surprised and pleased Charlotte and Gertie would be with the doll. She could hardly wait to get home.

All at once, quite out of the blue, a twinge of guilt pierced through her gloating. What about Mama? Think she'll be pleased, too?

No, she won't. Mama will be good and mad. Papa, too. I'll get a licking for sure. And this time I guess I deserve it. I'm a cheat . . . and a thief, too! I took charity, even though I know how Papa and Mama feel about that!

Henny's feet started dragging. What was she to do? How was she to explain it all to Mama and Papa?

You could take the doll back, conscience prompted.

Oh, no, I can't, I just can't! It would be awful, just too embarrassing.

You'll have to. It's what Mama will make you do, anyway.

Slowly, Henny turned and began retracing her steps. The late afternoon sun was already lost behind the tenement rooftops. An icy gust of wind pounced on a pile of papers and sent them swirling past her legs. Henny shivered a little and pressed the doll closer to her.

As she neared the end of the block, she noticed a little girl on a stoop. She was sitting all alone, bundled up in an old shawl. Henny paused and eyed the forlorn figure. It's so cold, and all she's got on is that old shawl. Full of holes too — real holes.

The child lifted her head and stared at Henny with eyes that seemed much too big for her wan face. The poor little thing . . . I bet she never had . . . instantly Henny knew what she had to do.

"Here!" She thrust the doll at the child.

The little girl crouched unmoving. Disbelief and wonder chased each other across her face.

"It's all right I tell you. Go on! Take it!" Henny ordered harshly. She pushed the doll onto the child's lap and fled.

"Hello, everybody!" Henny sang, trying to sound off-hand. She sped through the kitchen. Now, if she could just make the bedroom safely, she'd change into another pair of stockings before Mama could catch her. Somehow she'd get rid of the telltale pair.

But, alas, there was Mama planted in the doorway of the bedroom. "What have you done to your stockings?" she demanded.

It's no use, Henny realized ruefully. Mama has eyes in the back of her head. She looked down at her mangled stockings. "They got ripped."

"By whom?"

Henny's shoulders lifted in an I-don't-know gesture.

"I suppose the little elves did it," Mama said with a frown.

Henny made a grimace. Mama always said that when the girls wouldn't admit to something.

The remark set the other sisters to giggling. Henny glared at them. Did the whole family have to get in on this?

"Henny, I asked you a question!" Mama spoke sternly.

For a moment Henny's thoughts went darting about, furiously trying to make up a plausible story. But somehow her heart wasn't in it. She'd had more than enough of lying for one day. And all the trouble it had brought upon her! Now, all she could do was to tell the truth and get it over with.

So the whole story came tumbling out.

To Henny's astonishment Mama remained silent. Her sisters, too, were no longer giggling. For a little while, Mama seemed to be lost in thought. Then she turned to Henny and said quietly, "At least you knew you did wrong, and you tried to correct it. But I'll still have to tell Papa about it."

Henny groaned inwardly. That meant a licking for sure.

But strangely, Henny never did get the licking. Nor did she ever hear another word about her escapade.

4: Street Scene

SARAH SAT on a swing in the playground of the park. She swung idly, her feet barely skimming the ground.

Henny came sauntering over. "Let me climb up behind you," she said. "I'll pump for you."

"Promise you won't go too high."

"All right, scaredy cat."

Sarah moved over. It was pleasant having somebody else do all the work. Now if only Henny would stick to her promise. Sarah never did like to swing high; it made her feel funny.

But not Henny. The higher she went, the better she liked it. "Isn't it swell!" she shouted happily, as she pumped away. Forward — she bent her knees sharply. Backward —

she stood up straight, every muscle taut. How she loved the sudden rush of cold air, the feeling of flying free, up and away from the ground. "Whe-e-ee!" she sang out. Higher and higher flew the swing, the iron chains creaking and quavering a little tune as they strained at their ring bolts.

"Henny! That's high enough!" Sarah warned.

"Just a little more," coaxed Henny.

"No, Henny, please! No more!"

"Oh, don't be such a fraidycat! I just want to touch the roof once, that's all. Hold your feet up."

"No! I don't want to! I want to go down!" Sarah pleaded. Her stomach was beginning to act up. "I want to get off! I want to get off!"

The rooftop was rushing toward them. Sarah shut her eyes tight. Frantically, she clung to the iron chains. Now the swing was falling backward and Sarah's stomach turned a somersault. They were flying upward again! Maybe this time the swing would turn over altogether! A wave of nausea rolled over her. "Henny, I feel sick! Please—please, take me down!" her cries swung back and forth.

Ella was sitting on a bench nearby watching the baby. She heard Sarah screaming. "Henny," she yelled sharply, "slow down that swing this instant!"

"Aw—all right," Henny said grudgingly. She stopped

pumping and soon Sarah's toes were scraping the ground. Sarah sobbed with relief. It was wonderful to feel the world standing still again. Somewhat shakily, she wobbled over to join Ella on the bench.

"She looks positively green!" Ella cried anxiously. "You're not going to throw up, are you?" She turned upon Henny. "You know Sarah can't stand swinging high and yet you have to go and be so mean! Here, wet my handkerchief at the drinking fountain and bring it right back."

"Aw, she's always getting sick, or something," muttered Henny. "She belongs on the baby swings with Gertie." She squirmed uncomfortably. Sarah really did look sick, and it was all her fault. She rushed to the fountain and in a minute was back with Ella's handkerchief dripping cold water. Very contrite by now, she stood by and watched Ella bathing Sarah's face. "Want a lemon drop, Sarah?" she asked, fishing it out of her pocket. "It'll make you feel better."

"Thanks," Sarah said. She sucked away while both sisters studied her face intently. Slowly the green faded away and a faint touch of pink crept into her cheeks.

Henny breathed easier. "You're all right now, aren't you?" she said.

Sarah nodded.

"Want to go on the slide with me?" Henny offered.

Sarah shook her head. It was heavenly just to sit still.

"It's just as well," Ella said. "We have to go home. Go get Gertie and Charlotte."

They had walked a few blocks when all at once, out of nowhere, a gang of young boys appeared, their arms a jumble of bananas, apples, and grapes. Down the block they ran helter-skelter, whooping and shouting. Suddenly their leader glanced back. "Cheeze it!" he yelled in warning. The boys began to race like mad, bumping heedlessly into the passersby, dropping some of the fruit in their haste.

From around the corner a peddler came running. "Stop! Stop them!" his hoarse voice bellowed.

Like nimble monkeys the boys scattered, scrambling around pushcarts and wagons, slipping through the grasp of those who tried to catch them. A few moments more and the whole pack had vanished.

"They ran around the corner!" Henny exclaimed, jumping up and down excitedly. "Why doesn't somebody go after them?"

By this time shouts and angry voices filled the air. The girls turned toward the middle of the block where a crowd was rapidly forming.

"C'mon! Let's go see what's happening!" Henny yelled.

"With the baby carriage?" Ella asked.

"Oh, leave it there!" Henny told her, impatiently. "Nobody'll steal it. Especially with a baby in it."

Ella wavered for a moment. "No, I'd better not!" she decided. "You go and — "

The sisters did not wait for her to finish. They were off like a shot. Henny elbowed her way through the crowd. The grown-ups moved aside good-naturedly till finally the girls stood where they could see and hear everything.

In the center of the onlookers was the hoarse-voiced peddler holding fast to a young boy. He was twisting in the man's grasp, struggling to break away. "Lemme go!" he kept shouting. "I didn't do nuthin'!"

"I won't let you go!" the peddler stormed angrily. "You steal my fruit! I get a cop!"

At the word "cop," the boy's face blanched. But there was no hint of fear in the defiant tone of his voice. "You go call a cop! He can't do nuthin' to me. I didn't do nuthin'."

"Say, that's the boy who bumped into us in Papa's shop!" Henny said.

"The one who sells Papa things?" whispered Sarah. "It couldn't be!"

"I tell you it's the same boy," Henny insisted.

"Just wait till we tell Papa," Charlotte declared. "Won't he be surprised."

"Papa thinks he's such a nice boy, too," added Henny.

"Maybe he was hungry," Sarah said sympathetically. "Anyhow, who are you to talk, Henny? You snitched something off a pushcart once yourself."

Why did Sarah have to bring that up? Henny winced uneasily. "Aw, I only took a banana, just for a joke. That

wasn't really stealing. And anyway, Mama made me take it right back and apologize to the man." Henny gave a little shiver at the memory; it had been a hard thing to do. She regarded the boy with new understanding.

"You see this boy," the peddler was declaiming excitedly to the people around him. "He's no good! He belongs to a gang. They come by my stand. They steal my fruit. This is not the first time. Lotsa and lotsa times before, they steal my fruit!"

"Shame!" an old woman remarked. "They don't even let you make a living these days."

"Loafers! That's what they are!" a man put in.

"Kids like that ought to be locked up."

"That's right, Giuseppe, why don't you take him to the station house? The police will know how to handle him."

Giuseppe shook the boy vigorously. "I'll do what the people say!" he shouted. "I'll take you to the station house!" He began to push the boy before him.

"I'm not going to no station house!" the boy protested. "I didn't steal nuthin'. And I don't belong to that gang!"

"Then how come you were right here with them?" someone asked.

"I was not! I was just passing by."

"Liar!"

The boy's eyes flashed. "I'm not a liar! I never even saw any of those boys before."

The people looked at one another uncertainly. It was hard to know what to believe. The boy sounded sincere. And then again . . . he was ragged and thin. "The boy looks hungry," a housewife muttered. One could forgive a hungry child.

"I didn't steal nuthin'!" the boy kept repeating. "You gotta believe me! I didn't steal nuthin'!"

Henny couldn't bear it another minute. All these people picking on one little boy! The way he looked and spoke, you could just tell he wasn't lying. Why wouldn't they believe him? "I believe you," she cried aloud, "even if they all don't!"

All eyes now turned on Henny, but she did not waver. She stood her ground like a small fighting cock. Her voice grew shrill. "My Papa knows him. And me and my sisters know him, too. If he says he didn't steal anything, then he didn't. He comes to my Papa's shop lots of times, and my Papa says he's a nice boy. And my Papa knows. I just wish my Papa were here right now. He'd make you let him go!"

The sisters were embarrassed but in their hearts they felt proud of Henny. They gathered close to her.

"I think you're right, Henny," spoke a firm, steady voice.

Heads turned and necks craned to catch a glimpse of the speaker.

"It's Miss Carey! Miss Carey, from the settlement

house!" People smiled and made way respectfully. "Let Miss Carey through."

"What's your name, boy?" Miss Carey asked quietly.

The tousled head of dark curly hair turned upward. The frightened eyes moved swiftly over Miss Carey's face, but there was no answer.

"That's Guido," Henny blurted out.

Miss Carey put her hand on the boy's shoulder. Her voice was gentle. "Guido?"

"Miss Carey," the peddler interrupted, "I don't like to make trouble — but this boy — I think he's no good . . ."

"I understand, Giuseppe," Miss Carey replied. "It's an outrage that your fruit was stolen. But I believe Guido. I have the feeling he is telling the truth. Those other boys," she added, "are a problem that we at the settlement house are very much concerned about. But I'm sure, Giuseppe, you wouldn't want an innocent boy to be arrested."

Giuseppe shrugged his shoulders. "Well, maybe I got the wrong one." He released his grip on the boy's arm, but his voice rose. "All right now, but if I ever catch you stealin' my fruit . . ." He shook his fist threateningly in the boy's face.

"Thank you very much, Giuseppe," Miss Carey said,

quickly taking one of Guido's hands in her own. She looked around at the crowd. "May we get by, please."

"Guido, I don't believe I've ever met . . ."

Before Miss Carey had a chance to finish, the boy wrenched himself free and fled swiftly down the block.

"Want me to catch him for you?" a man asked.

Miss Carey shook her head. "No," she replied. "No — let him go." Her face clouded over as she watched him disappearing in the distance. She turned to Henny. "That was quite a speech you made. Did you say your Papa knows him?"

"Yes. He sells my Papa all kinds of junk."

"I see. Well, Henny, tell your Papa I'll come over soon and talk to him about the boy." She smiled at the children, nodded to the grown-ups, and moved off quickly.

The children watched her go. "Imagine that Guido," Henny said thoughtfully, "and Miss Carey so nice to him, too."

"Come on. Let's go tell Ella," suggested Charlotte. "She must be dying to know what happened."

5: *Purim Jester*

ELLA SCOWLED at the kitchen clock. Why did its poky old hands have to drag along so slowly? Didn't they realize how anxious she was to get to Hebrew school? "For heaven's sake," she cried out, "won't it ever get to be two o'clock?"

"Maybe if you stop watching the clock so much, it might go faster," Mama replied.

"Oh, Mama, just think, if I got the part of Queen Esther! Imagine playing the part of a real queen!"

Immediately she began imagining — a dazzling white gown — a golden crown studded with jewels on my head, and my long black hair floating freely around my shoulders. Proudly she lifted her small head. With all the grandeur of a queen, she advanced in slow procession across the kitchen floor.

Mama watched her with a mixture of pride and amusement. "Better not count your chickens before they're hatched," she advised.

"Oh, Mama, it's such a wonderful part! And I know I could do it! Mama, I just have to get that part! If I don't, I'll die!"

Mama shook her head reprovingly. "Ella, such talk!"

"I wish I were old enough to act in the Hebrew school plays," Sarah said wistfully. "Why don't you try out for a part, Henny?"

"Not me!" Henny cried. "Mr. Rosen expects you to rehearse every single day!"

"It's almost two o'clock, Ella," observed Mama.

"At last!" Ella exclaimed. She snatched up her hat and coat, her sisters' shouts of encouragement trailing after her. "Good luck!" "Hope you get the part!"

"All the male parts have been given out," Mr. Rosen said, "now let's get to the females. Let's see—for the role of Queen Esther . . ."

Ella could feel the increased tension in the auditorium—the swift intake of breath—the shifting about in the seats. She looked around at the many eager faces, her heart fluttering between doubt and hope.

"Dora, you first, please." Mr. Rosen motioned.

Ella listened intently as Dora read. Nothing to fear from her, she told herself. Dora could never play the part of a queen.

Sophie, Bertha, Lily—one after the other attempted the role. None of those girls are particularly inspiring, Ella concluded.

The lines rolled off the contestants' tongues. Ella had to battle with herself to keep from acting out the queen right there in her seat. Please, please, Mr. Rosen, me next! Let me try!

But the prayer went unheeded.

"Rachel!"

A tall, dark-haired girl came forward.

Rachel really looks the part, Ella had to admit as she watched her move gracefully onto the stage. Anxiously she listened. Rachel reads well, Ella thought jealously. But her innate honesty would not permit any clouding over of her judgment.

Still, she would not let her hopes wither. I'm sure I could do as well. Perhaps even a bit better. Mr. Rosen could at least give me a chance to try before he makes up his mind. She jumped up. "Mr. Rosen, please," she cried out, "couldn't I try too?"

Mr. Rosen regarded her thoughtfully. "But, Ella, there's another part that I've been saving especially for you. You're

exactly what we need. You're so little and cute, and you sing so well — the jester!"

"Oh, no, Mr. Rosen," Ella pleaded, "I want to try out for Queen Esther."

"That's not for you, Ella." Mr. Rosen was emphatic. "The jester — now there's a part that's just made for you!"

Ella felt as if her insides were suddenly scooped out. She could see it was no use arguing with Mr. Rosen. His mind was made up and nothing she could say was going to change it. It was the jester or nothing. She could not possibly bear being nothing. A sob caught in her throat. She fought it, even managing to bring a wan smile to her lips.

The feet that had skipped down the stairs so gaily just a few hours before now could be heard dragging upwards.

"I guess that's Ella!" Henny yelled, flinging open the door. She shooed her sisters back. "Make room for the queen!" she announced.

"I'm not," Ella murmured. There were tears in her brown eyes.

A blanket of gloom settled over the kitchen. Gertie gave voice to what they were all thinking. "Ella's not in the play," she wailed.

"Oh, I'm in the play all right," Ella assured them.

"So that's fine!" Mama said relieved. "That's fine!"

"Only someone else will be Queen Esther." Her voice grew mocking. "Me — I'm too little — too cute for a queen — that's what Mr. Rosen says. Besides, he needs me for a singing part. It's just perfect for me. Oh yes — perfect all right — the jester!"

"The jester!" all repeated in surprise.

"What's a jester?" Gertie asked.

"A jester is someone everybody laughs at," Ella explained bitterly.

"But in olden times, a jester was very important to a king," Sarah cried. "Whenever the king was tired or troubled, he could always depend on the jester to cheer him up. I think that's a wonderful part!"

"Of course, it is," declared Henny. "I'd a million times rather play a part that will make people laugh. You'll have loads of fun. And anyway, what could you do with a queen? Just walk around with your nose stuck up in the air."

"And the jester always wears such a gorgeous costume, with all different colors, and little bells tied on," Charlotte said.

"And he tells jokes and riddles. And sings and dances," Sarah added enthusiastically.

Mama nodded her approval. "Yes, Ella, I agree with Mr. Rosen. You will be very good in that kind of a part."

"Jester Ella — Jester Ella!" Gertie chanted, making it sound like a little song.

Ella looked around at her family. How wonderful they all were! She had dreaded coming home, ashamed to admit that she had failed to get the part. Now all the sore spots of her hurt pride were being smoothed over, melting away in the warmth of the family's enthusiasm. She opened her arms wide and gathered in as many of her sisters as she could. Her heart was bursting with love and gladness. "You'll see!" she cried. "I'll be the best jester Mr. Rosen, or anyone else, has ever seen!"

For Ella, the days took wings. She could talk of nothing but the Purim play and Mr. Rosen. There was the time she came bursting into the house with flushed face and shining eyes. "Mama," she gushed, "Mr. Rosen is just marvelous! The best director the Hebrew school ever had! Of course he's very particular but you don't mind because he's so patient. Do you know what he did today? He spent a whole half hour just teaching me how to turn my wrist so that when I point my finger, it should look graceful.

Can you imagine! He's so good-looking, too. All the girls have a crush on him." A tiny smile played around Ella's mouth. She wouldn't say anymore, but you could tell it had something to do with Mr. Rosen.

At last it was Purim. Throughout the day, the girls romped in their homemade masquerade costumes. From door to door they went, bringing Purim plates full of good things to eat. In exchange they were given other goodies and most often a few pennies.

But the high point of this Purim holiday came, when, in the evening, the family found seats in the auditorium of the Hebrew school.

"We have to save a seat for Miss Carey," Henny said.

"For Miss Carey?" Mama repeated. "How did she ever find out about the Purim play?"

Henny grinned. "I told her. And when she heard that Ella was going to sing in it, she said she'd love to come. So, I invited her."

Mama turned to Papa. "Isn't it nice that she takes such an interest in our girls."

"Oh, Miss Carey's interested in everybody," Henny replied with a shrug of her shoulders.

Papa nodded. "That's so. She came to visit me in my shop the other day to ask about the Italian boy."

"She did?" Sarah cried. "She said she would."

"Only there wasn't much I could tell," Papa went on. "He's a boy that doesn't like it when you ask him a question. Maybe when he gets to know me a little better . . . . Anyway, I promised her I'd see what I could find out. She seems like a fine lady, that Miss Carey."

"Look, Ma," Henny pointed, "there she is now! Yoo hoo! Miss Carey! Right over here! We saved you a seat!"

"Henny, shush!" Mama cautioned. She beckoned smilingly to Miss Carey.

"Well, now, isn't this thoughtful of you," Miss Carey said, settling herself comfortably in her seat. "I was afraid I wouldn't make it in time. I was busy teaching a new mother how to take care of her baby. That's always a pleasant job but it took longer than I expected." She looked around with interest.

"Miss Carey," Gertie spoke up, "the whole family's here 'cepting the baby. I'm glad I'm not the baby and have to stay home with a neighbor to take care of me."

Miss Carey smiled down at her. "I don't think the baby minds." She turned to Papa. "Have you been able to find out anything more about Guido?"

"A little more. One of the peddlers who is also Italian was in the shop when Guido came in. They spoke to each other in Italian and I guess that made the boy feel more at home. Anyway, we found out that he is an only child. His father is dead. His mother works in a garment factory."

"Did he mention where he lives?"

Papa shook his head. "I couldn't find out."

"I've made a number of inquiries myself," Miss Carey said, "but I haven't been able to find out either." She grew silent. All about them the children and grown-ups were laughing and chatting together, but for the moment, Miss Carey seemed to have forgotten where she was.

Suddenly there was an outcry from Gertie. "Oh! Oh!" She jumped up and began hopping up and down on one leg.

"What's gotten into you?" asked Mama.

"I got pins and needles in my foot!"

"Your foot went to sleep," Miss Carey explained. "It'll wake up in a minute."

"You shouldn't sit on it," said Charlotte.

"But then I can't see."

Papa folded his coat into a neat bundle and put it on Gertie's seat. "Try it now," he said, settling her on the coat.

Gertie looked around triumphantly. "Now I'm taller than anybody. I can see everything."

"Ssh," whispered Sarah, "it's starting!"

The lights dimmed. The audience grew still as a piano

struck up a rollicking tune. Slowly the curtain went up. There in the center of the stage stood the jester arrayed in a splendid red, yellow, and green costume.

"That's Ella!" Gertie squealed in delight.

The jester bowed, and a cluster of tiny bells on her peaked cap jingled merrily. With a wink to the audience, she began to skip around the stage, twirling a stick adorned with gaily-colored streamers.

A loud chord! She danced forward and began to sing:

> *Fol-dee-rol-dee-diddle.*
> *Can you guess a little riddle?*

The jester turned her head to one and all with a questioning air.

> *A king, a crown*
> *A prince's frown.*
> *And a terrible Jew who won't bow down!*

As she ended her song, she pranced around with such grace and spirit, the audience was captivated. A shower of applause followed her as she strutted offstage.

"Is that all?" Gertie asked, disappointed.

"Of course not!" whispered Charlotte. "That's only the introduction. Now the real play begins."

All through the next hour, the audience laughed, and wept, and worried along with the characters. But the most enchanting moments were those when Ella was on the stage. She leaped and twirled, and turned somersaults. She mocked at the villain, mimicking his voice and gestures. She amused the king with her songs and witticisms. One could hear favorable comments buzzing all over the auditorium. "That little jester!" "She's some actress!"

The final triumph was Ella's too, for she sang the song that ended the play. Her beautiful, strong voice rang through the hall, clear as a bell. "Such a little girl with such a big voice!" someone said aloud. The audience clapped and clapped till their hands ached. The curtain kept squeaking up and down as the players kept bowing and smiling and bowing again.

"Whose child is that little jester, I wonder?" a voice spoke up from somewhere behind the family.

Papa's face shone. He stood up and turned toward the questioner. All the pride in his chest burst forth in an exultant shout. "That's my daughter! My daughter!"

"Papa! Please!" Mama tugged at his sleeve, her face red as a beet.

"It's all right." Miss Carey smiled at Mama. "He has every reason to be proud."

6: Business of the Bath

"MAMA, are the things all set for the baby's bath?" Henny asked. "I'm ready to bathe him."

"Oh, no, you won't!" rejoined Ella. "It's my turn. You did last Sunday."

"I know. But I'm much better at it than you. Even Mama says so."

Oddly enough that was true. Harum-scarum Henny was really wonderful with the baby. On Sundays, when Mama let the older girls bathe him, she handled him so surely, you'd think taking care of babies was the easiest job in the world. Mama said no grown-up could be more careful or more gentle then Henny.

"I don't care!" Ella insisted. "I'm not going to give up my turn."

Henny appealed to Mama. "Wouldn't you rather have me do it?"

"No, Henny," Mama replied. "Ella has to have her chance, too."

"Now, Henny, don't you dare ask me to give up my turn next week," Sarah added quickly, "'cause I'm not going to. I have to learn, too."

"How about me, Ma," clamored Charlotte. "When will you let me bathe the baby?"

"When you're old enough."

"But, Ma, by the time I get old enough, he'll be all grown up and want to bathe himself."

"Me, too!" echoed Gertie.

"Well," exclaimed Mama, laughingly, "it looks like I'll have to borrow an extra baby for each one of you."

"Aw, shucks!" Henny flung herself down on a chair and sulked. But not for long. Her face suddenly brightening, she said, "Say, Ella, I'll trade you—a penny for your turn."

"You haven't got a penny," Ella replied.

"I have, too," retorted Henny. She slid her hand into her pinafore pocket and brought out a shiny copper penny. "See!"

Ella looked at it suspiciously. That couldn't be today's penny. Mama never gave out the daily penny allowance until after lunch. And it just couldn't be yesterday's. Everybody knew Henny couldn't keep a penny from one day to the next. She had to rush right out and spend it. As Mama said, "Money burns a hole in Henny's pocket."

"Where'd you get it?" Ella asked.

"Oh," Henny said evenly, "from someone. Well? Yes or no?"

The sisters looked first at the penny and then at Ella. Would she let herself be persuaded? You could buy lots of interesting things for a penny.

"No!" Ella was firm. "No trade."

Henny shrugged her shoulders. "I guess they'll just have to be satisfied watching you bathe him."

"We'll be satisfied, all right," said Sarah.

"Oh, I don't mean you, silly," Henny told her. "I mean my friends."

"Your friends? What have they got to do with it?" demanded Ella.

"I promised a couple of my girl friends that they could come this morning and watch me bathe the baby," Henny explained.

"Henny, you didn't!" Mama exclaimed with dismay. "It'll upset the baby to have strangers around."

"But, Mama, they're only girls. The baby is certainly

used to having a lot of girls around. I just couldn't say no, Mama. They begged me to let them come. Right now, none of them have any little babies around the house and I felt sorry for them."

"But you could at least have asked me first, Henny," Mama protested. She had no time to say anything more for from outside the kitchen door came the sounds of shuffling feet.

"That's them now!" Henny cried. She opened the door and a swarm of girls came barging into the kitchen. The sisters greeted each visitor hilariously, but Mama just stood by aghast and counted. There were Dora, Fanny, Tessie, Esther, and Goldie — five in all! Mama threw up her hands. "Henny! Is this what you mean by a couple?"

Henny pretended she hadn't heard. All at once she was very eager to be helpful. "I'll get the baby's tub," she called out and whisked out of the kitchen. She was back in no time, the tin tub sitting like an enormous pear-shaped hat on top of her head.

By now the visitors had grouped themselves in an admiring circle around the baby's high chair, oohing and ahing. They rumpled the baby's silken hair. They cooed baby talk at him. Any other infant might have been startled by all this attention, but not Charlie. He smiled broadly, his

baby fingers reaching out to grab a stray lock of hair or a too inquisitive nose. And all the while his bright eyes examined the strange faces with interest.

Henny poked her head out from underneath the bathtub. "Say, you girls," she shouted above the din, "we're getting ready. I thought you came here to watch."

"Of course." "Can we help." "What shall we do?" the five girl friends responded eagerly.

Henny stole a glance at Mama. Mama certainly didn't look any too pleased. Ten girls in one room did sort of clutter things up a bit. Now if they all hovered around Mama, she'd be knee-deep in kids. Then she might get real mad. "No.

You're just to watch," she informed her playmates. "That was our agreement — just to watch!"

"Oh, all right," the newcomers consented grudgingly.

Mama helped Ella lay out the baby's clean clothes on a blanket spread over the kitchen table. Next to them they placed all the toilet articles needed for the baby's bath.

"Henny," Mama asked, "how long are you going to march around with the tub on your head?"

Quickly Henny's head came out from under, and she set the tub down on the kitchen floor.

It's a toy boat, Gertie decided, and it's inviting me in. She climbed in and sat down, all hunched up, knees bumping her chin. "Look at me, everybody!" she cried. "I'm a baby. Who wants to give the baby a bath?"

Gertie wiggled around. "See, I'm rocking the boat," she said, swaying the tub from side to side. The tub teetered on its rounded bottom. Then kerplunk — crash! It fell over to one side, spilling Gertie onto the floor. Everyone but Mama laughed boisterously.

"Now the tub will have to be carefully scrubbed before we can use it," Mama said severely, but somehow her voice sounded as if there was a laugh hidden in it.

The tub was taken to the sink and thoroughly scrubbed, then half-filled with warm water. Meanwhile, Henny and

Sarah prepared a stand by placing two chairs face to face. Then they helped Ella carry the tub from the sink to the stand. Into the tub went a couple of large diapers folded lengthwise. Ella smoothed them carefully. "You've got to have something soft for the baby to lie on," she informed the visitors. Then, folding several diapers into neat squares, she placed them in the upper, wider part of the tub. "This will be his pillow."

She rolled up her sleeves and touched one bare elbow to the water. "It feels just right." Next she lifted the baby from his high chair and placed him on the blanketed table. The children crowded around so they could watch Ella undress him.

Ella felt a bit nervous with so large an audience observing her every move, but she tried hard not to show it. Finally, the baby was ready. "Out of my way!" she ordered. She picked him up and lowered him cautiously into the bath. Gently, she began splashing the warm water over his tummy. The baby broke into a big smile and stretched his chubby legs.

"Oh, he's so darling!" the visitors cried. "He loves it!" "He's laughing all over himself!" They shoved one another trying to get a better view.

All this excitement made the baby very playful. His

little hands slapped at the water. His legs pumped steadily up and down. He gurgled with delight and pumped even harder. The water churned and jumped up into the air, spraying over faces and clothes. Everyone drew back, screeching. "I'm soaking wet!" yelled red-haired Dora. "You'd think I was taking a bath!"

With the girls' milling around in the wet, the floor was soon a muddle-puddle. Mama took one look and shook her head despairingly. With a sigh, she turned to the kitchen stove and busied herself with the pots.

"You've played long enough, you rascal you," Ella said. "Now you're going to have something you don't like. You're

going to have your head washed."

The visitors crowded in still closer. "I can't see from way back here!" protested Charlotte.

"And I can't see either," Gertie complained.

"What do you have to see for?" Henny demanded. "You've only seen it done a hundred times before. You're supposed to be polite to your guests and give them a chance."

Charlotte pulled up a kitchen chair and climbed up on it. "C'mon up here, Gertie," she called out. "You can see fine from up here."

Quickly, Gertie scrambled up after her.

Ella felt more nervous than ever. Washing the baby's head was the hardest part. Carefully she rubbed a soapy lather over his head. She was doing very nicely when Goldie accidentally jostled her arm. Ella's hand slipped forward over the baby's face. His eyes screwed up tight and he let out a howl.

"Oh, you clumsy thing!" Henny yelled. "You've got soap in his eyes!"

"Oh, the poor darling!" "It stings him!" "Oh, poor, sweet baby!" All the girls were in a panic. "Quick, wash it out!"

Mama was there in a moment. Pushing Ella aside, she washed and rewashed the baby's eyes with warm water, murmuring soothingly all the while. "There, there! Mama'll get the soap out. Yes, I know. It burns."

Ella stood by unhappily. Henny was right. She was clumsy. Now maybe Mama wouldn't let her finish the job.

However, the baby's sobbing quickly died down. "Mama," Ella said miserably, "I was careful, but with so many people all pushing and shoving, I could hardly move."

"I know it wasn't your fault," Mama assured her. "Don't worry. See, he's all right now."

Indeed the baby had stopped crying and was once more his own smiling self. Ella breathed a sigh of relief.

"I think you'll be able to finish the job now," Mama said. "I'm going in to change the sheets in his cradle so he'll be ready for his nap."

Mama went into the bedroom and again Ella took over. "You girls make it awfully hard for me," she said. "There are really too many of you. Why don't you give me a little more room?"

"Look, we want to see," Esther said.

"Sure. What do you think?" Fanny cried. "I'm all crushed up as it is. I gotta twist and turn every which way to get a look."

"Hey, get your arm out of my way, Fanny!" exclaimed Tessie. "I paid a penny, too, you know!"

"Here, Tessie," Henny whispered quickly, "take my place." And she left the group altogether.

The sisters exchanged glances. Then they turned and eyed Henny. She made believe she didn't see them.

"Dora," Ella asked, "did you pay a penny, too?"

"Of course. We all did," Dora replied. "Henny said we couldn't come otherwise."

Ella exploded. "Henny! Of all the . . ."

"Ssh . . . please! Here comes Mama," begged Henny.

The sisters said nothing further but they all looked daggers at her.

The bath proceeded without further mishap. "There," Ella said finally, "you're as clean as a whistle." She sent the warm water splashing in small waves over the baby's body. "You like that, don't you?"

"Please, Ella, let me splash him," Goldie pleaded.

"Ooh, let me!" "Let me!" the others joined.

"With your dirty hands!" cried Ella. "No, sir!"

The visitors examined their hands; they really weren't too clean. "If we wash them, then can we play with him?" asked Esther.

"I think the baby's been in the tub long enough," Mama interposed. "Bathing tires him, you know," she explained to the disappointed children. Lifting the baby from the tub, she wrapped him snugly in a large towel. "Wet babies are pretty slippery," she went on. "That's why my girls let me take care of this part."

When the baby was dry, Ella dressed him rapidly. "Such tiny clothes!" exclaimed Tessie. "I bet they'd just fit my big doll."

"Well, he's just like a big doll," Charlotte told her proudly.

"Oh, he's better than a doll," Gertie chimed in. "He's alive! He's a live doll!"

"But why does he have to wear a dress when he's a boy baby?" asked Esther.

"All little babies wear dresses. It's easier to put on and take off," Ella said.

She brushed the baby's hair. Then she curled his front hair around her finger. Soon the baby had a long rolled curl perched on top of his head.

"Stop it, Ella!" Henny cried. "You're making him look like a girl! Now that we finally have a boy in the family, do you have to make another girl out of him?"

"Oh, leave it, Henny," her friends all insisted. "He looks so cute this way."

"I'm training it. So it'll be wavy when he grows up," Ella said. "Girls like men with wavy hair."

"I guess the baby is all ready for his nap," Mama announced. "He must be pretty worn out with all this fuss." And she carried him off to his cradle.

Everybody helped in cleaning up the mess in the kitchen, and soon it was time for Henny's friends to leave. "It's so much fun around here," Fanny said enviously, "with a baby and everything."

"Could we come again and watch?" Esther asked.

Mama nodded. "Yes, you may, but please, not all at one time."

"Thanks," said Dora. "And do we have to arrange it with Henny first?"

"Why, no," said Mama. "Just come."

"Good-bye! Good-bye!" The visitors trooped out of the kitchen and started down the stairs.

"Wait for me!" Henny shouted after them. She was gone before anyone could say "boo."

Ella gathered her sisters around her. "Are we going to let her get away with all that money?" she whispered.

"Certainly not!" they whispered back.

"Then come on, quick!" Ella commanded.

"What in the world!" Mama wondered as she watched her daughters fly out of the kitchen like a whirlwind.

Henny was just about to enter Mrs. Blumberg's candy store when her sisters caught up with her.

"You've got some nerve!" Ella cried, all breathless from running. "The baby isn't yours. He belongs to all of us. When you get paid for showing him off, you have to share with all of us!"

"That's right!" agreed Charlotte.

Practical Sarah had it all figured out. "You had five visitors. A penny apiece means you got five cents. And we're just five. So if you give each of us a penny, it'll come out just even."

"But that's not fair!" stormed Henny. "It was my idea. None of you would ever have thought of it!"

"Hmm. I wonder how Mama would like your little money-raising scheme?" mused Ella.

Henny scowled. "Oh, all right," she said. She took out four pennies and distributed them among her sisters.

"Oh, goody!" squealed Gertie. "C'mon everybody! Let's go in and buy some candy!"

Ella Lends a Helping Hand

7:

IT WAS AN unusually warm Sunday for May. The girls lolled on the front stoop, basking in the bright sunshine. Charlie was playing happily with his bare toes in the baby carriage.

Henny was admiring her new cotton stockings. "Thank heavens we don't have to wear those awful woolen ones anymore. I'm glad it's spring."

"Is that why it stays light so long?" asked Charlotte. "because it's coming close to summer?"

"Uh huh," Henny answered. "I wish it were summer already."

"Not me," said Sarah. "I don't care for summer. It's so hot and I miss school."

"Oh," Henny cried, "imagine anyone missing school! And especially homework! I can't wait till it's over so I can play all the time."

"Which reminds me," Ella said. "How about returning my ball and jacks? Sarah and I want to play with them."

"I haven't got them. I loaned them to Goldie."

"Well, you can just go and get them back," ordered Ella.

"Oh, don't be so stingy. You'll get them back. She only borrowed them for a little while."

"Yes, but we want to play now." Ella was getting indignant. "You had no business lending out my ball and jacks in the first place."

"Well, you see, Ella, Goldie gave me a pickle from her father's stand. I had to pay her back in some way. Now that I ate it all up, I can't ask her to give them back right away, can I?" Henny smacked her lips in memory.

"You might have at least saved me one little bite," Ella said.

"I meant to. Honest I did," Henny replied remorsefully. "But I took one bite and then another. Now that I think of it, it must have been an awfully short pickle. Because before I knew it, the whole thing was gone."

Everyone burst into laughter. "Okay, Henny." Ella

jumped up, still laughing. "I'll tell you what. I'll go by the pickle stand myself. I'm sure Goldie's all through with the ball and jacks by now."

Henny grinned. "Goldie's very good-natured. Maybe she'll give you a pickle, too."

But Ella never got to the pickle stand. She had walked about a block when she came upon a slight boyish form staggering under the weight of two large bundles. It was Guido. He would have passed her by but she planted herself right in front of him. "Hello, Guido!" she called.

"Oh — hello," he said uncertainly.

"You don't remember me," Ella went on. "But it was my sister Henny who stuck up for you the other day." She looked at him reproachfully. "And you never even bothered to say thank you."

Guido stared down at the ground. "It sure was swell — your sister and that lady sticking up for me. I shoulda — but all those people . . ." He shifted his bundles uncomfortably. "Well — anyhow — thanks. So long."

"Wait a minute! You can't carry those bundles all by yourself. Let me help," Ella urged.

"No. They're too heavy for a girl."

"I can manage," Ella assured him, taking hold of one of the bundles. It *was* heavy. How in the world was he able to carry two of them? "Say," she asked, "what have you got in there — rocks?"

"Pants," answered Guido unsmilingly.

"Pants? You work in a clothing store?"

Guido shook his head. "They're from the factory. My mother used to work there all day on a sewing machine. Then she got sick and it got too hard for her. Now she does finishing at home. You know — sewing on pockets and buttons and things like that. I bring the bundles home and then take them back to the factory."

Ella glanced at him as the words came tumbling out. She noticed his eyes. They were all red as if maybe he'd been crying. What was wrong, she wondered?

"Gimme the bundle!" Guido exclaimed suddenly. "I gotta go."

But Ella wouldn't give it up. "Let me go with you."

Guido frowned and turned his head away. He's trying hard not to cry, Ella said to herself. She stood still and waited.

"It's on the Bowery," Guido said finally. "It's quite a ways from here."

"I don't mind," replied Ella.

They walked in silence for several blocks; then suddenly Guido spoke. "My mother hasn't been feeling good for a

coupla months. Now she's much worse — just lying down
most of the time. Couldn't do no work at all this whole week.
I gotta take these pants back unfinished."

"Gee, I'm sorry about your mother, Guido. Who's taking care of her?"

"Nobody but me."

"Don't you have any relatives?"

"No."

"Can't you get someone to help out?"

"We don't know anybody. And anyway my mother
doesn't like anyone to know when things are bad."

The city blocks stretched out endlessly. Ella's bundle

grew heavier with every step. She was glad when they sat down on a stoop to rest. She did not ask any more questions. She kept looking at Guido's face, longing to say something comforting.

Guido stood up, picked up his bundle and said gruffly, "C'mon. Let's go."

They walked the rest of the way without exchanging another word. Finally, Guido said, "This is the Bowery. The factory's across the way."

Ella had never been on the Bowery before. She gazed about curiously. High overhead was the elevated train. On either side, a narrow single track ran close to the upper stories of the houses, leaving the center of the street open to the sky. The strong sunlight filtered through the spaces in the tracks, forming crosshatched designs on the sidewalks below.

They crossed the street, dodging the numerous horse-drawn vehicles clattering over the cobblestones.

Ella would have liked to stop and rummage through the merchandise in a secondhand store. Or at least, to look through the window of a pawnshop with its fascinating array of trinkets and valuables. But Guido hurried her along — past the restaurant on whose windows the menu and prices were painted in white chalk — past the saloon through whose swinging doors there streamed the sour, sweet, bitter smell of beer and free lunch.

"This is the place," Guido said. He led the way into a narrow dingy hallway, and they trudged up the rickety, wooden stairs. On the second floor, Guido opened a door and a tremendous roaring sound filled Ella's ears. Even the very walls seemed to tremble. "What's that?" she exclaimed.

"Sewing machines," Guido told her. "Electric ones."

They entered a long room which ran the entire length of the building. It was crowded with machines, tables and people. On the floor, mounds of garments were piled high. Near the far end, between two grimy windows, Ella could see a long cutting table. Two men, with tape measures dangling from their shoulders, were pinning a brown paper pattern to a bolt of cloth spread out before them.

The room was hot and close. Men and women operators sat hunched over the sewing machines, beads of perspiration running down their faces. Ella watched their expert fingers guiding the material as it flew under the whirring needles. The floor was littered with scraps of cloth, cord, paper, colored thread, and pins. Here and there, electric bulbs covered by green metal shades hung suspended from the ceiling. They shivered with the rumble of the machines, setting their circles of light dancing on the factory floor.

A train rolled by, its pounding clackety-clack adding to the confusion of sound. The cars seemed to sway perilously close. Ella shouted into Guido's ear, "I bet if I stretched my hand out of the window, I could shake hands with the conductor."

Guido smiled slightly. He approached one of the cutters with his bundles. Because of the noise, Ella could not make out what was being said, but she saw the man shake his head sadly as he took the bundles from him.

Guido signaled to Ella and slowly the two left the factory and walked down the stairs.

The family was about to sit down at the table when Ella came in.

"Well, how do you do," Henny greeted her. "And how many pickles did you eat?"

"I never even got to see Goldie."

Mama regarded Ella. "Where were you?"

"Remember Guido? Well, I was with him." She turned to Papa. "He's in trouble."

"Again! What did he do now?" Henny asked.

"No. It's his mother. She's been sick for quite a while. But now she's much worse." Ella described her visit to the factory, repeating all Guido had told her about his mother and himself. "Guido's so worried. He doesn't know what to do."

"The poor boy," Mama murmured.

Ella continued. "Guido even stopped going to school so he could help out at home. But now with his mother so sick and not being able to work at all, they don't even have enough money for a doctor or medicine. Not even for food!"

"There's no one they could turn to?" questioned Papa.

"He said they had nobody."

"Not even a neighbor?" Mama exclaimed.

"I asked him that, too," replied Ella. "But he said they hadn't been living in that tenement very long."

"Mama, what do you think? Maybe you ought to go over and see how things are," Papa suggested.

"I think it's a good idea. I'll go over with Ella as soon as we finish eating. Papa, you'll see that the children get to bed, and Henny, don't forget to give the baby his bottle."

Supper was a quick affair. Afterward, while the girls cleared away, Mama got ready to go. Silently they watched her fill a large paper bag with a jar of chicken soup, some bread, a couple of eggs, and a glass of her own prune conserve. "It's not much," she observed.

Papa pulled out his well-worn purse from his trouser

pocket. He unsnapped it, counted out a dollar's worth of change, and handed it to Mama. "Here," he said, "maybe you'll need it."

Dusk had fallen when Mama and Ella came downstairs. The narrow ribbon of sky above had turned a deep blue, and dark shadows already lay on the old tenements. Down the block, the lamplighter was busy with his long pole. One by one he turned on the gas mantles in the tall lampposts, sending out bright greenish-yellow streams of light on the darkened streets. A few peddlers were wearily pushing their carts before them. Here and there, men in shirt-sleeves, and women in house dresses, sat on the stoops, chatting, while small groups of children played noisily in the gutters.

They had not gone far when Ella said, "It's somewheres on this block." A moment later she pointed to a house next door to a stable. "This is it."

The stable doors were open and from its interior, there poured forth such a strong overpowering horsey smell, Ella had to hold her nose.

They entered a long, narrow hall. Walking past the stairs that circled upward on the left, Ella pushed open the back door which led into a gloomy, littered yard. At the far end was a second building. "A yard house," Mama remarked.

Above them, flickering rays of light skipped from the open windows onto washlines full of clothes, that crisscrossed from one building to the other. Several cats were rummaging in the open pails and boxes. From a pipe which ran up the side of the house, rusty-colored water dripped and settled into a dark brown puddle.

They crossed over the cracked slate walk to the rear building. Inside the hallway was so dark, they had to grope for the staircase. Up and up they climbed. From behind closed doors, they could hear a baby wailing, loud voices speaking in a foreign tongue, and an occasional snatch of song.

At last they came to the top floor. "Five flights!" gasped Mama, as they stopped to catch their breath.

"Last door to the left, Mama," Ella directed.

Mama knocked. There was the sound of running feet and the door opened. Guido stood in the doorway. "Hello, Guido," Ella said. "I brought my Mama."

"Come in," he answered.

In the darkness they could make out a small, shabby room almost bare of furnishings. In one corner, on a cot, lay a thin, motionless figure.

Guido lit a candle.

"Never mind that," Mama said, putting her parcel on the only chair in the room. "I'll put a quarter in the gas meter." She held a match to the gas jet. There was a sudden sputter and a pale, yellowish light spread over the room.

Mama knelt down beside the cot. The sick woman's cheeks were feverishly red, the skin drawn tight over the cheek bones. Feebly she turned her head and a pair of large, luminous eyes, so like Guido's, stared up at Mama.

Mama put her hand on the woman's forehead. "It's all right," she said gently, stroking the tangled hair. Then she stood up. "Ella," she whispered, "go right over to the settlement house and see if you can get Miss Carey. Tell her we need a doctor. Tell her it's for Guido's mother."

When Ella had gone, Mama heated her chicken soup in a worn pot she found on a shelf. She coaxed a few spoonsful into the woman's mouth. The woman struggled to speak. "Is good — but — please excuse — no more." She closed her eyes, and her hands dropped limply over the thin coverlet.

Mama put the rest of the soup on the table with a thick slice of bread and the preserves. "Sit down, Guido," she said.

He shook his head.

"Now, Guido," Mama was firm, "if you want to help your mother, you must eat — to keep up your strength."

Guido needed no further urging. By the time Ella was back with Miss Carey, he had eaten everything laid before him.

"The doctor will be here shortly," Miss Carey said. She set her nurse's bag down on the table. Her eyes moved swiftly about the neglected room and came to rest on Guido. A faint shadow of pain crossed her face.

She seems upset, Ella thought, watching her.

For a long minute, Miss Carey continued to look at the boy. Then she came over to him. "Guido," she said softly, "why don't you wait downstairs for the doctor."

Guido hesitated.

"You don't have to worry about your mother," Miss Carey added. "We'll do everything we can for her."

"I've seen many such places in my work," Miss Carey remarked to Mama in a sad voice after Guido left. She drew herself up. "Well, there's a great deal to do," she said briskly, rolling up her sleeves. "Let's heat some water so I can get the patient clean and comfortable. Then we'll do the room."

Miss Carey tended the woman all by herself. But when it came to tidying up the house, she insisted on helping Mama and Ella. Mama marveled as she watched her scrubbing the sink. When she remarked about this, Miss Carey replied matter-of-factly, "Dirt breeds germs," and went right on with her cleaning.

By the time Guido was back with the doctor, everything was shipshape.

The doctor greeted Miss Carey and nodded to Mama and Ella. Pulling out a big handkerchief, he mopped his brow. "Whew! Those stairs! Well, now, what have we here?"

The examination was brief. Anxiously, Guido hovered near. The doctor put a hand on the boy's shoulder and addressed Mama. "Are you a relative?"

Mama shook her head. "No. We just came to help."

"I see." The doctor rubbed his chin. Then he spoke

directly to Guido. "Listen, boy, your mother is very sick. She has to be taken to the hospital."

"To the hospital?" Guido repeated. His face grew pale. He pulled away from under the doctor's arm and ran to his mother's side.

Miss Carey knelt down beside the boy. "Guido, we're only trying to help. You want your mother to get the best of care, don't you?"

Guido did not reply. He put his head down on the coverlet and wept.

Ella's hand sought Mama's, pressing it hard. She felt choked with tears.

The doctor, too, cleared his throat. "You'll stay here, of course, Miss Carey, till the ambulance comes."

"Yes, doctor."

"Well, then, I'll be on my way." He snapped his bag shut. A quick nod to Mama and Ella, and the door closed behind him.

The room was quiet. Miss Carey still knelt beside Guido. The sick woman turned her face to her. Her eyes were full of worry. She put her hand out weakly and touched Miss Carey's sleeve. "My Guido, who take care my Guido?"

"I will. I'll take care of him."

The worry faded from the mother's eyes. She sighed.

"Guido — he good boy — " Her voice trailed away.

Later, downstairs, they all stood wordlessly by as she was carried into the ambulance. They watched the driver take up the reins and slap gently at the horses. "Giddap!" He kicked his heel down hard, and the bell underneath the foot rail rang out — clang, clang, clang! it sounded in warning and people scurried out of the way. The wagon wheels began to turn, the bell never ceasing its clamor. Faster and faster they revolved, and soon the ambulance blurred into the far distance.

Ella could not bear the bewildered look on Guido's face. "Don't you worry, Guido," she said as cheerfully as she could. "Everything will be all right, you'll see."

Miss Carey turned to Mama. "I'm so grateful you called me. I'll take Guido to the settlement house for tonight."

Mama slipped her arm through Ella's. "Come, Ella."

Mutely they walked along the dusky streets. "You know, Mama," Ella broke the silence. "I can't help but wonder about Miss Carey. Looking at her, just listening to how she talks, you realize she comes from a very different kind of background. She must have been brought up by people who were well to do, don't you think? What do you suppose made her take up nursing in the first place? And then to come down here to the East Side to work with the poor! It's hard to understand."

"Not really," Mama answered. "There are exceptional people in this world whose hearts are big. They really care about what happens to others. It's people like that who started the settlement house. They work out of concern for others with little thought for their own comfort or the money they might earn. And Miss Carey — well, that's the way she is."

Neither spoke again until they had reached home. Then Mama said, "We're lucky, our family. We're all well — and happy — and together." She started up the stairs. "Yes," she repeated, "we're certainly very lucky!"

The Wrong
Side of
8: *the Bed*

HENNY FELT herself getting crosser by the minute. She squirmed restlessly in her seat. Would the class never end? Was Mama right? Had she gotten up on the wrong side of the bed this morning? She frowned. Which was the right side, anyway? She knew that when she had first awakened, she had felt fine. She remembered dancing around in her petticoat, singing at the top of her voice:

> *Two more weeks and we'll be free*
> *From this school of misery.*
> *No more pencils, no more books.*
> *No more teachers' saucy looks.*

Mama had told her to shush. "Henny, you're making

too much noise. And besides, Mr. Basch doesn't like your dancing on his head so early in the morning." Somehow after that, everything had gone wrong.

For instance, she was crazy about Charlie. She had only wanted to give him a hug. But she must have squeezed a bit too hard for he howled, and Mama had scolded her.

Then Charlotte was mooning around, and she couldn't resist playing a trick on her. She pulled the chair out from under her just as she was about to sit down. Even now, cross as she was, Henny couldn't help chuckling at the picture of an astonished Charlotte sprawled on the floor. Only – Charlotte had cried. She said it hurt. Again, Mama was angry. She had spoken very severely. "Henny, that's very dangerous! If I ever catch you doing it again, you'll get a wallop!"

And then there was breakfast. Fresh, crusty rolls piled up in the breadbasket just out of reach. She just wanted to get one for herself. So her cup of cocoa had to be in the way of her elbow. Of course, it spilled all over her clean pinafore. Mama had made her change it – not without another scolding.

Then just when it was time to leave for school, she couldn't find her history book. She hunted everywhere. Mama, too. It grew so late, her sisters left without her. At last, Mama found the missing book in the baby carriage.

"Henny," Mama had cried in exasperation, "of all places to keep a school book!"

She had tried to explain. "I put all my books in the carriage yesterday when we were playing downstairs. I guess I just left the history book there when I – "

"So, of course, you didn't do your history homework." Mama was grim.

"Ma, it's almost the end of the term anyway," she had protested.

"Still time for your teacher to make you left back!" Mama had retorted.

Naturally all this hunting for a stupid old history book had made her late. Another scolding – from the teacher this time.

Henny heaved a big sigh. How dull it was in the classroom! She was sick of sitting up straight with her hands behind her back while Miss Corbett's voice went on and on about geography. Henny's eyes darted restlessly over the room. Blackboards needed a good washing, she decided. They were grayish with chalk. The pussy willow branches had yellow flowers sticking out all over. It's awful hot in here, she thought, even with the windows open. She fanned her curls up and down.

How could anyone expect you to keep your mind on

schoolwork when it was such a lovely day? She wiggled about impatiently. If only there were something to do instead of listening to this boring stuff!

Her lips seemed shut, her face expressionless, but all of a sudden a shrill little squeak piped out into the room from somewhere back in her throat. Miss Corbett stopped talking and looked around. There was silence.

"Open your readers to page 116," she said.

A loud rustling of pages and everyone was ready for the reading lesson. Miss Corbett was just about to say something when she heard it again — the same little squeak. Her head came up sharply. She scanned the faces of the children. Her eyes stopped suspiciously at Henny, but Henny's face looked so innocent, she couldn't be sure. "Fanny," she said after a moment, "will you please stand up and read the paragraph at the top of the page."

Behind Fanny's protecting back, the squeak came again, louder this time. There were a few delighted titters.

"Who's doing that?" Miss Corbett inquired sternly.

There was no answer, and from the faces, it was impossible to tell. Miss Corbett was annoyed. "Go on with your reading," she ordered.

Fanny went on. The class fidgeted expectantly. Would

the naughty one dare do it again? She'd have to be extra careful. Miss Corbett was watching now.

Nothing happened for a while. Fanny finished her reading and Miss Corbett called on the next pupil. Her eyes turned back to her own book.

And then it came again, over and over.

"Teacher, there must be a mouse in the room!" yelled Fanny in mock alarm, jumping up from her seat.

"There it goes!" Henny shouted and began scrambling under the desks for the imaginary little visitor. Now from under the desks the squeaks came—louder and squeakier.

Miss Corbett rose from her chair and strode up the aisle

toward Henny. Arms folded, she stood still and waited. Henny's blond head popped up and just as suddenly the squeaking ceased.

Miss Corbett glared at her. "Henrietta," she exclaimed, "you've tried my patience long enough! Now you march yourself right down to Miss Phillips' office this minute!" "Oh!" "Poor Henny!" Excited whisperings flew through the room. "She has to go to the principal's office!" "I'd be scared to death if it was me!" "Maybe they'll throw her out of school altogether."

Henny flounced out of the room with her head high. Nobody was going to know that she was really quaking with fright. Aw, what are you scared of, she kept steeling herself. All Miss Phillips will do is give you a lecture or put you in a baby class for a day or so.

Bravely she entered the principal's office. The room was empty. She walked over to a window and stared out. Leaning her elbows on the windowsill, she cupped her face in her hands. The sunshine played on her blond curls, making them glow with light. If only I were a bird, she wished, I'd fly right up into the sky. I'd fly away, forever and ever, and never come back.

She was so busy imagining herself a bird, she did not

hear Miss Phillips come in. She started as a voice behind her said, "So much gold in the hair! What a pity there's so little in the heart!"

Miss Phillips studied Henny's stubborn little face. No use trying to talk to the child now, she decided. She sat down at her desk and wrote out a brief note which she slipped into an envelope. "Henrietta," she said, "you will give this note to your mother. I've asked her to come to see me tomorrow." She hesitated a moment. Her face softened. "You may go back to your classroom now."

Henny jammed the note into her apron pocket and stalked out of the office. Angry tears scalded her eyes. She dashed them away. Only babies cry, she told herself fiercely.

At the classroom door, she gave herself a little shake. All right now, she whispered, and flung open the door. At once, all heads turned in her direction. All they saw was a proud little girl with a devil-may-care grin on her face. "Miss Phillips sent me back," she called out, walking jauntily to her seat.

The lessons dragged on. When at last the dismissal bell rang, Henny rapidly gathered up her books.

"Just a minute, Henrietta." Miss Corbett's voice was severe. "You're not to leave with the others. You will stay

here until you've written the words 'I'll never make noises in class again' one hundred times on the blackboard. Rest of the class dismissed."

Henny slammed her books down on her desk. When teacher's back was turned, she stuck her tongue out at her. That made her feel a mite better.

Henny wrote and wrote and wrote. Her arm began to ache and the lines became more and more wavery. But all the time, the anger inside her bubbled and boiled. This was just too much. Nobody likes me, she said to herself glumly. Nobody ever does anything nice for me. Even at home there's nothing but scoldings and punishments—sometimes even spankings.

I'm going to run away. Just run away some place where they'll never find me. That will make them all good and sorry! And it would serve them right for the way they treat me!

Finally the dreary task was completed. She pressed the chalk down on the last word so hard it broke in her hand. Throwing the pieces on the floor, she ground them with her heel, delighting in the powdery mess she made. Then, picking up her books, she fled from the room.

She was outside at last. Where should she go? She walked along slowly, her mind busy with an exciting idea. When next she looked up, she found that her feet had led her home. There was no one around. Tiptoeing through the hall, she stole into the backyard. She raced across the yard straight to an empty sugar barrel which stood in a corner. Throwing her books inside, she climbed in after them. She heaved a deep sigh of contentment as she curled up on the barrel bottom. It was cozy and quiet in here. Nobody would ever dream of looking for her inside the sugar barrel. She pulled out her library book and began to read.

All that afternoon, Henny's sisters romped in the park playground until suppertime.

"Mama," Charlotte said as the girls thronged into the

kitchen, "You should see how Charlie loves the baby swings. We had some job getting him off. He made himself stiff as a board, and hollered!"

"We'll have to take him more often," Mama said, smiling at the baby.

"Henny home yet?" Ella asked.

"No," answered Mama. "Wasn't she with you?"

"Fanny told me she had to stay in after school," Sarah disclosed.

"Oh, no," cried Mama. "What's it this time?"

"Henny made noises and all the children giggled," Sarah said. "Henny's awfully funny sometimes. You have to laugh even when you know you mustn't."

"I don't imagine it's so funny for the teacher," commented Mama. She glanced at the clock. "Would she be keeping her this late?"

"She's probably gone over to Fanny's house," Ella said. "Don't worry. She'll be here when it's time to eat."

But when Papa came home, Henny still had not shown up.

"Mama, did you go to the hospital today?" Papa asked. "Did you see Guido's mother?"

"I was there, but they wouldn't let me see her."

"Why not?"

"They said she was too sick for visitors."

"Not even Guido?" Ella asked.

Mama shook her head.

Nobody said anything for a while. Everyone was feeling sorry for Guido. Then Mama spoke. "Well, children, supper's ready. We won't wait for Henny."

It was supper hour. From all around, through open windows, out into the backyard, and down into the barrel, there floated the tantalizing smells of cooking. Slowly Henny stood up, all cramped and stiff. I wonder what Mama is having for supper? Fried onions. Scrambled eggs with onions — with the delicious pumpernickel bread — with lots and lots of sweet butter. Mmm! Henny pressed her hands hard against her tummy. It felt so empty. From all sides, she could hear the sounds of voices, the clink and clatter of dishes. She sighed and squatted down again. Suddenly she felt very lonely. She stared up at the rim of sky above her. It'll be dark soon, but I'll be safe in my nice strong barrel, she comforted herself. Soon her head leaned against the barrel's side and her eyes closed drowsily. The next moment she was fast asleep.

In the kitchen, Papa was saying, "Where is that child? Doesn't she know she's supposed to be home at suppertime?

What she needs is a good spanking."

Mama was beginning to worry. Henny liked her food too much to forget when it was suppertime. "Ella," she said, "as soon as you've finished eating, I want you to go over to Fanny's house and see if she's there."

"I'm all through, Ma. I'll go right now." Ella hurried out of the kitchen.

Soon she was back. "She's not there. She hasn't been there all afternoon."

Now Papa began to worry, too. "You think maybe she went to the library?" he asked.

"Oh, no," said Ella. "She wouldn't go today. Friday's our library day. And besides, the children's room closes at six o'clock. It's way past that now."

"Maybe she went to the settlement house to see Guido," Sarah suggested.

"Want me to go there, Mama?" asked Ella.

"Yes, and Charlotte, you run downstairs and ask Mr. Basch if he saw Henny this afternoon."

Papa put on his jacket. "I'll just have a look around," he said.

One by one the family returned with no news. One by one Mama sent them out again to comb the neighborhood. They hunted everywhere – in the homes of friends and relatives, in the school yard, at the Hebrew school, near the city parks. Word of the missing Henny brought the neighbors flocking into Mama's kitchen with all kinds of suggestions.

"Did you look in the backyard?" someone asked.

Immediately a host of faces peered out of the windows. "By night, you can't see a thing out here." "Henny!" "Henny, you out there?" voices shouted.

Henny woke with a start. She rubbed her eyes. She couldn't remember where she was. Somebody was calling her. Instantly it all came back to her. Her heart pounded. She squeezed herself into a tight ball trying to get lower in the barrel. They mustn't see her. She held her breath, listening. But no one came near. The voices gradually faded away.

Just think of it, exulted Henny, all this fuss about me! Now that I've gone, I bet they're awfully sorry. Well it serves them right!

But her elation did not last long. Time passed slowly. Nothing else happened. She was getting restless. It was so hard to sit still for so long. By now her body was one big ache. If only she could stretch her cramped legs. She twisted and turned, but it didn't help. It was very dark now, even with the stars out. Hugging herself tightly, she shut her eyes against the darkness.

All of a sudden, on the back fence, a cat screeched. Henny jumped. She could feel the hair standing up on the back of her neck. She ran her hands up and down over her bare arms. "Ooh, it's chilly," she murmured. And I'm so hungry, I could eat up a house. Anyway, by now Mama and Papa must be terribly worried. I bet the girls are pretty scared too. All on account of me. Well, maybe, I guess, they've all been punished enough. And besides, I don't like that old cat. Not in the nighttime. I think I'll take pity on them after all. I think I'll go in.

Stiffly she climbed out of the barrel. For a whole minute, she kept rubbing her cramped legs. Then she collected her books, smoothed out her wrinkled dress, and walked toward the hallway.

Inside the kitchen, the children were huddled around Mama. Gertie was crying. "Mama, do you think she was run over and taken to the hospital?"

"Maybe she was kidnapped!" exclaimed Charlotte.

"Kidnapped!" The word was tossed about by the neighbors. "The child could have been kidnapped. Who knows?"

"You should go to the police station," someone said. "After all, when a child gets lost, that's the first place to go."

Precisely then, the door opened and Henny came swaggering in. "Hello," she announced cheerily. "Ma, what have you got to eat? I'm starved!"

Everyone stared at Henny in astonishment. Excited questions rained down on her from all sides. "What happened?" "Why are you so late?" "Where were you?"

"Oh, just around," Henny replied.

"Henny!" It was Papa. His tone was ominous.

The neighbors exchanged glances. They nudged one another and began to leave hurriedly.

As soon as the door closed, Papa walked over and lifted the strap from the kitchen wall. Henny cringed. The children held their breath. She was sure going to catch it this time!

But over their heads, Mama's eyes met Papa's. Reluctantly, Papa's arm came down. The girls sighed, relieved. Henny was not going to get a licking after all.

Without a word, Mama laid out the remains of supper, and Henny fell to. "By the way, Ma," she said, between huge mouthfuls, "I think the principal wants to see you tomorrow. She gave me an invitation." Henny pulled the crumpled envelope out of her pinafore and handed it to Mama.

That night Mama and Henny had a long, long talk.

9: *Hijinks at the Settlement*

"YOU KNOW, girls," Mama remarked, "Guido's mother has been at the hospital for a whole week now."

"How is she, Mama?" Ella inquired.

"I went over there last night, but they still wouldn't let me see her. They say she's too ill. I think it would be real nice if someone went down to the settlement house to see Guido. He must be very lonely."

"Let's all go," suggested Henny.

"Yes, let's," the sisters agreed.

So that afternoon they walked to the settlement. Miss Carey was busy writing at her desk but she put down her pen as soon as she saw the family.

"Hello, everybody," she said warmly.

"Miss Carey," Ella said, "Mama knows she can't visit Guido's mother right now but she was wondering if she could send her something like soup or stewed fruit, maybe."

"How very kind and thoughtful of your Mama. But you can tell her I'm not sure it would be allowed at this time."

"Is Guido here?" Henny asked. "Can we see him?"

"By all means. You'll probably find him sitting around in the playground. The poor boy is terribly unhappy. We've all tried but we just can't get him to do anything. Most of the time he just sits and broods. You're such good company, maybe you can cheer him up."

"That's really why we came," Ella said.

"Is Guido going to stay here?" Sarah inquired.

"No," answered Miss Carey. "He'll be leaving for our summer camp in a few days."

They were walking down the stairs to the backyard when Henny suddenly stopped. "Listen, everybody!" she whispered excitedly. "I know how we can help Guido." They drew together in a huddle while Henny outlined her plan. Five heads were better than one and soon they all had good ideas to add. Such chitchat and giggling that went on! Finally Ella clapped her hands. "Now quiet all of you! And no laughing! We don't want him to catch on. And remember, everyone waits her turn. I'll tell you when."

They made their way through the crowds of laughing, shouting children to where Guido sat slumped forlornly on a bench. They lined up before him. "Hello, Guido!" Ella sang out gaily. "Meet the family."

Guido nodded his head moodily.

"Okay, Gertie," Ella said under her breath, "you're the first."

Gertie stepped forward as her sisters drifted away. Ella, Sarah, and Charlotte sat down under the wistaria vine that grew along a trellis, while Henny ran over to the parallel bars where the bigger boys were showing off.

Gertie pulled on Guido's sleeve. "Guido, I want to walk on the fence. Will you lift me up?"

"Walk on the fence?" Guido repeated questioningly.

"Yes. I want to walk all the way around." She took hold of his hand.

"Get one of your sisters."

"But I want you to do it. Please, please, Guido."

"Aw, go lift yourself up."

"It's too high."

"Well, stand up on one of those little green chairs."

"But I have to hold on to your hand while you walk me around."

"Will you stop pestering me!"

Gertie squeezed her eyes together and opened her mouth wide. She let out a piteous howl. "Wah, waah! Guido doesn't want to let me walk on the fence! I never once walked on the fence! All the other girls have. Waah!" She kept tugging at his arm and crying as if her heart would break.

Guido was getting more and more uncomfortable. At last he could stand it no longer. "All right, all right! I'll do it. Only stop that yammering!"

From different corners of the yard, the sisters grinned at one another. "You know, Sarah, I think Gertie's as good an actress as Ella," Charlotte declared.

Perched on the fence, her hand tight in Guido's, Gertie kept teetering along, shouting in triumph, "Hey, look at me! Look how big I am!"

The fence was rather high. "You be careful or you'll fall!" Guido warned as he staggered along, trying to keep her steady.

Ella motioned to Sarah. "As soon as Gertie gets down, I'll go next."

With a tremendous plop, Gertie jumped down from the

fence into Guido's arms. "Hey, watch out!" he cried, stumbling back, almost falling over.

Ella came running. "Never mind her, Guido." She grabbed his arm and pulled him onto a bench. She talked very rapidly. "Listen, Guido. We're giving a play in the assembly. I'm supposed to be an Italian woman. They gave me that part because I can sing. Now I thought it would make the part more real if I sang in Italian instead of English. I already know the tune of 'O Solo Mio' so I thought I'd sing that. But I don't know the Italian words. Will you write them down for me?" She shoved paper and pencil under his nose. "Please, Guido."

"I don't remember the—"

"Then sing it, Guido, and the words will come back to you."

"Sing it here?"

"Why not? You can sing softly so no one else will hear. Please, Guido! I'll sing it with you." She started to sing the melody. Surprised by the loveliness of her voice, Guido found himself listening. Rather shamefacedly, he recited the words while Ella hummed along.

"That's wonderful, Guido! Now write them down!"

Guido let himself be persuaded. Together they struggled over the words. They were only half through when

Charlotte dashed toward them, screeching loudly. She sprinted around behind Guido, grabbing hold of his shoulders. "Save me! Save me! Henny's after me!"

"Say, let go!" Guido struggled to get free. "Can't you see I'm trying to write something?"

Charlotte only clung the tighter. Right in front of Guido, almost on top of him, Henny was dodging from side to side. "You just wait till I get hold of you, Charlotte! I'll teach you to throw sand at me!"

"Well, you had no right to call me names!" Charlotte shouted back.

Henny made a grab for her. Charlotte ducked, and ran around the bench. "Ha, ha, ha! You can't catch me!" she taunted.

"We'll see about that!" yelled Henny.

Around and around they chased each other, banging into Guido at every opportunity. "Hey, take it easy, will you!" Guido cried, getting more annoyed by the minute. But they ignored him completely.

While all this was going on, Ella kept demanding, "Guido, please, what's the next word?" And Gertie was pulling on his sleeve adding her wail to the general hubbub, "I want Guido to walk me around on the fence!"

In desperation, Guido appealed to Ella. "Holy cats!

Can't you make those sisters of yours behave?" He stood up, bristling with anger. "Go on, beat it, all of you! If you have to fight, go and fight someplace else!"

"Guido's right," agreed Ella with a big wink to Henny. "That's enough!" To Guido's amazement, the two sisters walked off, arm in arm, apparently the best of friends, with Gertie tagging after.

Guido grunted, "Crazy kids!"

Ella chanced to glance up at that moment and was surprised to see Miss Carey watching at the window. She was shaking with laughter. I wonder how long she's been standing there, Ella thought. She looked down quickly so Guido wouldn't notice.

"Now that we have a little peace and quiet, Guido," she said, "let's finish the song."

Guido went back to his writing and pretty soon the job was done. Ella took the paper from him gratefully. "I just know this will make the song a big success. Thanks a million, Guido."

Over by the swings, Henny whispered a few words into Sarah's ear. Sarah nodded and ran over to Guido. She took out a rubber ball and tossed it up and down. "I bet you're a real good ball player, Guido," she started off. "I bet it would be fun playing with such a good player like you.

Could you throw the ball to me just once, Guido — boy's way? I'd like to see if I could catch it boy's way." Shyly she put the ball in Guido's hands and began backing up. "Is this far enough?" she cried out.

"More!" Guido ordered.

Sarah backed up again.

"Still more!"

"Can you really throw a ball that far?" Ella exclaimed.

For an answer, Guido stood up, raised the ball above his head, drew up one leg in real baseball style and let the ball fly. Whizz! It sailed across the yard, low and hard, through Sarah's outstretched hands, landing with a loud smack against her chest. "Oooh-p!" she gasped.

Guido came running over. "Thought you wanted it thrown boy's way, are you hurt?"

"No, I'm all right, Guido," Sarah assured him. "Boy, you sure can throw a ball!"

He was suddenly surrounded by the whole family. "Did you see that!" Charlotte cried in admiration.

"Some dandy pitch!" Henny enthused. "Wish I could pitch like that!"

"Girls can't pitch," Guido said with a superior air.

"Well, I can catch. How about throwing me a ball?"

Everyone watched as Guido threw a fast ball to Henny.

She really could catch. To Guido's surprise, she could pitch, too. "Not bad for a girl," he admitted grudgingly.

Henny returned the compliment. "Boy, could they use you on the Giants! You're the best pitcher I ever saw."

"Aw, that's nothin'. Come on over to the overhead ladder. I'll show you a good trick." Guido started off with the whole family prancing merrily behind.

At the ladder, he sprang up lightly, catching hold of the end rung with one hand. Swiftly, hand over hand, he traversed the ladder. At the final rung, he chinned himself five times midst a loud chorus of praise. Then he jumped down gracefully.

"You're wonderful!" "A regular acrobat!" "And look, he isn't even out of breath a teeny bit!"

Guido shrugged. "I can chin lots more times than that if I want to."

"That's hard to do!" Henny said.

"Yes," boasted Guido. "You need muscles."

"Think I could do it?"

"Well," Guido deliberated, "I don't know."

"Could you show me how it's done?"

"Okay. Watch." Once again Guido swung himself up and down. This time the girls counted out loud up to ten.

"Now you try it, Henny," her sisters said.

"Yeh, go on, try it," urged Guido.

In a trice Henny hung suspended from the ladder. "Oh! Oh!" she squealed, her legs churning wildly under her. Slowly, painfully, she began to pull herself up. "Is this how you do it?" she asked.

"That's good!" Guido encouraged. "Now let's see if you can pull yourself up again."

"I'm tired!" Henny exclaimed. But she chinned once more before she dropped to the ground.

"It pulls on your arms," she observed, "but it feels great. Thanks for teaching me, Guido."

"That's okay," Guido replied. "Anytime." By now he was all enthused. "Ever see anyone hang by the legs from the parallel bars?" he asked.

"No! Can you do that?"

"Sure. Just watch me!"

He would have gone on showing them every trick he knew but it was nearly closing time. Miss Carey came out to get Guido and bid the girls good-bye.

"I always knew girls were pests but these are the peskiest bunch I ever saw. I'm sorry for their mother. I bet they must drive her crazy." He laughed a little. "They're a lot of fun though."

"That they are, Guido," Miss Carey said, her eyes twinkling.

In the street five convulsed girls were walking home feeling mighty pleased with themselves. "Henny," Ella chuckled, "I've seen you chin a dozen times in a row as easy as pie."

"I know," replied Henny, giggling all over herself. "It was hard to keep myself back. But I had to let him beat me. Anyway, we sure made him feel a lot better, didn't we?"

10: Guests For Supper

ONE SUNDAY afternoon, the sisters were gathered in their usual spot in front of the house. Henny was pushing the baby carriage back and forth, back and forth, all the while cracking away in rhythm on a wad of gum.

"Wish I had some gum," Gertie said. "You got any, Ella?"

"No."

"Henny, how about giving me a piece of yours?"

"From my mouth?"

"I can wash it off."

"Nothing doing! Besides the sweetness is all chewed out already."

"I don't care."

"Well, you're not getting any."

"Never mind her, Gertie," said Charlotte. "I just remembered there's some gum I stuck under the kitchen table. Let's go get it."

"Look!" Henny suddenly pointed. "There comes the hurdy-gurdy! Ooh, they're stopping right on our block!"

Charlotte and Gertie jumped up and down joyfully. Baby Charlie, secure in his harness, stood up in his carriage and did a little jig of his own.

The hurdy-gurdy man and his little wife, wheeled their pianolike box to a spot right across the street from where they were sitting.

"Come on!" Henny shouted, pushing the carriage before her.

"Let's go, Gertie!" Charlotte cried as she and Sarah rushed after Henny.

"Gertie! You wait for me!" cautioned Ella.

But Gertie wouldn't wait. "I can cross by myself."

At the curb, directly in her path, stood the iceman's horse and wagon. Tiny Gertie didn't bother to go around; she calmly ducked under the horse and made for the other side.

"Gertie!" gasped Ella, horrified.

But by this time Gertie was safely across the street.

"What a crazy thing to do!" Ella scolded when she caught up with her.

Gertie looked up at her in surprise. "Why? I always go that way. The horses don't mind; they've got lots of room under their bellies."

"You're never to do that again!" Ella cried, shaking her finger in Gertie's face. "Suppose the horse kicked you or suddenly started to move? You could get killed!"

Gertie looked back at the horse dubiously. "All right, Ella. I won't do it no more."

The organ grinder turned the handle on the side of his music box as his wife stepped forward, shaking her tambourine invitingly. Thumpety-thump- dr-r-ring dr-r-rang, the melody rolled out. From everywhere children came scurrying, and even grown-ups gathered around to listen.

Catching hold of her skirt, Henny skipped about. Other children joined in and soon about a dozen little girls were whirling merrily. The organ-grinder grinned broadly and kept on cranking. A new, livelier tune burst forth. Quickly, the children chose partners. Hand on hip, the other curved gracefully overhead, they danced a spritely tarantella. To and fro went the couples, shaking their heads gaily and stamping their feet. And all the while the wife beat on her tambourine.

Many of the grown-ups hummed along with the music, and when the dance was ended, they applauded.

Tune after tune was played while the organ-grinder's wife wove in and out of the crowd, holding the tambourine before her. Out of purses, from knotted corners of handkerchiefs, the pennies came. Every so often, a shout from some

window high up in a tenement would bring her running.
Skillfully, she would catch the penny, wrapped in a wad of
paper that was tossed down to her. Each time a penny was
added to the small collection on the tambourine, she would
curtsey and smile her thanks. And as she bobbed forward,
two long strands of white hair which stuck out from either

side of her black straw hat, curtsied along with her.

At last there were no more pennies to collect. The organ-grinder lifted his hat gratefully. Then bending forward, he grasped the handlebars of his music box. With his wife pushing from behind, he slowly pulled it up the narrow street. Around the corner they went, a host of small youngsters tagging after.

"Whew, I'm hot!" cried Henny. "Say, the iceman's still here. I'm going to get me a piece!"

She ran over to the wagon. "Please Mr. Iceman, can me and my sisters have a teeny, weeny piece?"

The iceman pointed with his tongs to the glistening chips scattered on the wet floor of the wagon.

"Ooh, thanks!" Henny exclaimed, scooping up a handful. The wagon was immediately besieged by a mob of clamoring children. "Gimme! Gimme!"

"Gwan, beat it!" the iceman yelled good-naturedly. "Get off my wagon. I gotta go!"

Henny distributed a chunk each to her sisters and the rest into the nearest grasping hands. Back again on the stoop, five mouths sucked on the smooth icy bits.

"It's so cold, it burns!" cried Charlotte, hastily dropping her piece back into her palm.

"You gotta suck on it slowly," Sarah explained. "And you pull it in and out of your mouth like this."

Alas, all too soon, the ice was gone.

"What should we do now?" Henny asked.

"Ella, would you read to us from the book I took out from the library?" proposed Sarah. "It's the *Red Fairy Book*."

"Good," Ella agreed. "Go and get it."

Sarah was back in no time, hugging the precious book. "Mama says to read only one story. She wants us to come up early 'cause Miss Carey and Guido are coming to supper."

"Guido? That's a surprise," Henny said. "I thought he was supposed to be staying in camp the whole summer."

"He is," replied Sarah. "Miss Carey's just bringing him in so he can go to see his mother at the hospital tomorrow."

"If they're letting him see her, she must be getting better," Henny observed.

Ella's face clouded. "I don't think so. Mama tells me she has consumption."

"Consumption? What's that?" asked Gertie.

"It means her lungs are sick," Charlotte explained.

"Can you die from that?" Gertie quavered.

"Yes . . ." Ella's voice was very serious. She held up a

warning finger. "Now remember, when Guido is here, no one is to even mention it." She opened the book. "Well, let's get to the story."

The house was spanking clean, the table neatly laid, and the children washed up by the time the guests arrived.

"Everything shines so," said Miss Carey, looking around her admiringly. "I'm sure we could eat off the floor."

Mama beamed. "Thank you. We're so glad you could come. And Guido!" She shook hands with him. "My, my! How well you look!"

Guido flushed and stared down at his shoes.

The girls, too, regarded him with interest. Could this be the scrawny, unkempt boy they had first run into in Papa's shop? This Guido was definitely taller and neatly dressed in knickerbockers and a white shirt. His unruly black curls were brushed back from his forehead in smooth, shiny waves. His face was sunburned a healthy tan.

"I never realized what a good-looking boy he is," Ella whispered to Henny. "Such beautiful dark eyes and that wavy hair! He'll be some heartbreaker when he grows up."

All this scrutiny made Guido ill at ease. Hands dug in his pockets, he stayed close to Miss Carey. But the sisters' warm interest and lively chatter gradually began to draw him out. Soon he found himself responding to their innumerable questions.

"What's it like in the country?" Charlotte wanted to know.

"Okay."

"I bet there's lots of room to play there," Gertie put in.

"Yeh. When I first got there"—there was a small twist to his smile—"I wondered who had taken away all the houses."

Everyone joined in laughter.

"Are there lots of trees like in Central Park?" Gertie asked again.

"Way more. And there's a place to swim!"

Charlotte sighed. "It must be beautiful!"

"It's like a farm, isn't it?" stated Sarah.

"Well, there's a garden. With lots of flowers and vegetables, too. I like to work in the garden."

"Girls!" Papa interrupted. "Enough questions already! Mama, maybe it's time to start eating?"

For supper, Mama served some things neither Miss Carey nor Guido had ever tasted before. "This is sour cream," Mama announced, placing a small dish of the thick, white mixture before Guido.

Everyone watched while he took a little on his spoon

and carried it gingerly to his mouth. "It's really sour," he said after a moment. He looked as if he wasn't quite sure whether or not he liked it.

"Put some sugar in, Guido," Henny advised. "That's the way I always eat it."

So Guido added a little sugar. Around and around he stirred his spoon in the smooth cream. Reluctantly he took another taste. This time his face broke into a smile. "It's not bad this way," and he took a big mouthful.

"Wait, Guido." Charlotte stopped him. "You're supposed to eat it together with the blintzes. Mama made them especially."

"That's right," Mama said, setting a large oval platter on the table. Spread before them, in neat rolls, lay golden-yellow blintzes, flecked with brown buttery specks, their edges curling up crisply.

"What did you say these interesting looking things are?" asked Miss Carey.

"They're called cheese blintzes," explained Mama. "It's just sweetened pot cheese rolled up in a sort of pancake. Go ahead, try one," she urged.

Miss Carey took a bite. "Um. Delicious!"

The girls were being extra careful about their manners

today. Those nearest to Mama whispered in her ear if they wished a second helping. Those further away whispered to the next one and the message was carried down the line. They listened attentively when the grown-ups talked, and they did not interrupt. Mama was pleased. They're really well behaved, my girls, she thought.

But her glow of pride did not last very long. While the grown-ups were chatting, Charlotte had unfolded a blintze and gobbled up the cheese filling. Then she carefully smoothed out the pancake in her plate. It looks like a big yellow moon, she decided. All it needs is a face — like the man in the moon. Picking up the pancake in both hands, she quickly bit out two neat little holes at the top. There now — he's got two eyes. Now he has to have a nose — and she bit out a narrow slit. Last of all, out came a wide slice for the mouth. With a giggle, she plastered the man in the moon over her face.

Just then, Mama's eyes came to rest on Charlotte. "Charlotte," she cried out in embarrassment, "what will our guests think?"

Everyone stared at the mischief maker. But she looked so comical, they could not refrain from laughing. Papa, especially, laughed so hard, he had to wipe his eyes.

Supper over, the girls cleared away while Mama put Charlie to bed. Afterward the guests were invited into the front room.

"Ella, won't you sing something for us?" Miss Carey asked.

"All right. What shall I sing?"

"Why don't you sing 'Oiffen Pripetchik,'" suggested Papa. "It's an old Jewish melody, Miss Carey. It tells something about the life of the Jew in the old country. Jews were not permitted to attend regular schools, so they studied in a *chedar* — that means school. It was usually just a room in the house of the rabbi. When I was a child, boys began their study of the Torah at a very early age — four or five. A father taking his son to *chedar* for the first time would give him a little honey to taste. That's so the child would understand that learning and studying were sweet as the honey." Papa's face grew distant with remembering. "Winter mornings it was still dark when we boys started off for *chedar*. We carried lanterns to light our way. It was good to come in from the cold into the warmth of the schoolroom. Believe me, it was a long day. We studied till evening . . . well . . ." Papa shrugged away the memories. "Tell our guests what the words mean, Ella."

"That's all right, Papa," Ella replied. "I have an English translation."

Accompanying herself on the piano, she sang the English version:

ON THE HEARTH

On the hearth a little fire burns
And the house is warm
And the teacher has the little children
Learn their A—B—C's.
Listen children, remember precious ones
What you're learning here.
Say it once again and yet still once again
A—E—I—O—U.
When you children will grow older
Then you'll understand
All the sorrows in these ancient letters
And how many tears.

"That was lovely," Miss Carey said when the song was ended. "It's such a plaintive melody. Did you like it, Guido?"

Surprisingly, Guido was alive with admiration. "Gee Ella," he burst out, "I bet you could sing in the opera!"

"Oh, sure!" Ella responded with a wave of her hand. "How about you, Guido?" she countered. "How about singing another song?"

Guido smiled and shook his head.

"Oh, go on, Guido," everyone begged.

Henny took hold of his arm. "Come on, Guido. Don't be bashful." She pulled him toward the piano.

Guido shifted from one foot to another, then looked around with a shy little smile. "Well, if Ella will sing 'O Solo Mio,' I'll do something along with her."

Ella played an introduction, and with a nod to Guido, began singing. Guido joined in, and to the amazement of all, he was singing in harmony. He sang softly at first, gaining confidence as he went along.

"Guido, that was marvelous! It sounded just wonderful!" Everyone's delight was so evident, Guido flushed with pleasure.

"Who taught you to harmonize?" Ella asked.

"Nobody. I just do it. I don't have to think about it."

"That's a rare gift, Guido," Ella said. "You're really very musical. You ought to be studying."

Miss Carey nodded. "Maybe that can be arranged."

"Oh, Miss Carey, before I forget," Papa suddenly broke in, "one of the peddlers brought in a bundle of suits. From a fire in a clothing store. There's a boy's suit in the lot, a nice blue serge. How it got in there I can't imagine. It's certainly in first class condition. I think it's just Guido's size, too. I'd like him to have it."

"That's very generous. What do you think, Guido?"

"Thanks." Guido hesitated . . . "But I can't take it without . . ."

"Tell you what, Guido," Papa interrupted quickly. "It costs me very little. You take it now and you can pay me back later when you're working. How's that?"

Guido's face lit up. "That's okay."

"Then come over to the shop with me right now, if Miss Carey will excuse us, and you can try it on. Then you can be all dressed up when you go to see your mother tomorrow."

"You go right ahead," Miss Carey said. "We ladies will have a nice chat meanwhile."

"That's a fine boy," Mama remarked after Guido and Papa had gone.

"Yes, he is," Miss Carey replied fondly. "Living up at camp, working and playing with other boys, has done him a world of good."

"Yes. He seems so much more friendly," Ella said.

"Does he miss his mother?" Charlotte asked.

Miss Carey's voice grew gentle. "He doesn't say he misses her but he talks to me about her quite a lot."

"And how is she?" asked Mama.

Miss Carey sighed. "If only we had known sooner . . ."

"What's going to happen to Guido?"

"He'll stay on with me."

"At the settlement house?"

"No, he can't continue staying there. I now have a small place of my own."

Mama glanced at Miss Carey. "Guido's a lucky boy to have such a friend."

"Thank you. I guess I'm lucky too." Miss Carey's voice faltered. "He's lonely . . . and I . . . ."

Gertie nestled close to her. "Guido won't feel lonely with you," she said.

"You're very sweet, Gertie." Miss Carey hugged her tight.

Something hard pressed against Gertie's head. It was Miss Carey's watch. She drew back, examining it curiously. Her little fingers caressed the engraved surface. "You got a pretty watch," she said.

"Yes," Miss Carey said softly. "Someone gave it to me a long time ago."

Gertie pressed something and the watch snapped wide open. There were two photographs encased inside, one of a man, the other of a young boy. There was something familiar about the boy's face. "Is that Guido?" Gertie asked.

Miss Carey stared down at the open watch. "It's not Guido," she said abruptly. She took the watch from Gertie's hand and snapped it shut.

"What's the matter?" Gertie's high childish voice was full of concern.

Mama frowned. "Gertie!"

But Gertie did not understand. "Miss Carey, why do you look so sad?" she asked.

Miss Carey's usually strong, resolute expression was wistful. "That's a picture of my own little boy," she said. "He does look a lot like Guido. He was about the same age when the picture was taken."

"Your own little boy?" repeated Gertie.

"Yes dear, my own little boy." Miss Carey's eyes were rimmed with tears.

"But — but — where is he now?"

"He and his father are dead."

"Oh, Miss Carey!"

The clock on the mantelpiece seemed to tick extra loud. No one moved. Miss Carey went on speaking quietly. She kept looking straight at Mama all the while as if she were speaking to her alone. "Pneumonia. It was fatal to both of them." Her fingers clasped the watch tightly. "It was a long time ago — and I'm really Mrs. Carey. Afterwards, I made up my mind to become a nurse. So that perhaps I could help others to live." She stopped and turned her head away.

Impulsively, Mama came over and put her hand on Miss Carey's shoulder. Miss Carey smiled up at her. She patted Mama's hand reassuringly. "It's all right," she said. "Once we were a family of three. Now I have a very, very large family — the friends and neighbors whom I help — and who help me."

11: *Sarah Is Sewed Up*

SARAH WAS suddenly wide awake, feeling elated. Now why was that? She searched her mind a moment. Of course! This was the day when Uncle Hyman was taking her to the jewelry store! She sat up and looked around. Her sisters were still fast asleep. She listened. No sound from the kitchen either. Was Mama still sleeping, too? Goodness, it must be awful early.

Snuggling back under the blankets, she hugged her happiness to her. Then she found herself thinking about Uncle Hyman. She and her sisters often poked fun at his comical moon face and his too-short body and the way he stood with his feet turned way out. Sometimes we're awful mean about him, she thought regretfully. And he's all alone — with no wife and no children. He's so kind, giving us pennies and sometimes even presents. Like today — he's going to buy me a pair of earrings — real grown-up earrings!

Last Thursday Uncle Hyman had come for supper, bringing with him a gift of a dozen eggs. So as usual, Mama served him his favorite meal — four hard-boiled eggs and half a loaf of sour rye bread spread thickly with butter. When he had finished, he leaned back in his chair with a loud sigh of contentment.

"Sarah," he had said, "Mama tells me it's your birthday soon. Imagine! You, too, ten years old already! Well, when one of my nieces gets to be a young lady of ten years, she's certainly entitled to an extra special birthday present. Now what would you like I should get you?"

"Oh, Uncle Hyman." Sarah's voice was all eagerness. "Could you, please, buy me earrings? Like you bought Ella and Henny when they were ten years old. I've been wanting earrings for such a long time!" She stopped, abashed. "You said something special. Is earrings too much?"

Uncle Hyman had laughed. "If it's earrings you want, then it's earrings you'll get. I'll come over on Sunday and we'll go pick them out."

Well, today was *the* Sunday. Today they'd all go to pick out the earrings.

Did it hurt, she wondered. Ella and Henny said no —

but maybe they'd forgotten. She felt a trifle worried. Oh, well, she consoled herself, what does a tiny hurt matter when you get something wonderful in exchange.

Oh, how slowly the clock moved! But at last it was time to get up. At last Uncle Hyman arrived. At last the five girls hurried with Uncle Hyman across the street to Mr. Landau's jewelry store.

Sarah's excitement grew as she watched Mr. Landau pull out tray after tray of shiny earrings.

"I like this one. It's got such a big red stone," cried Gertie. "Take this one, Sarah."

"Oh, no," said Charlotte. "That's way too big. Little ones are much nicer."

"Say, look at these!" exclaimed Henny. "Real diamonds!"

"Not for a girl," Ella objected. "They'd be all right for a grown-up lady."

Then Sarah saw a small pair with a tiny blue stone in the center. How brightly the blue sparkled against the gold. "Oh, aren't they lovely!"

Ella nodded. "And the blue would look so nice against your blond hair. I wonder if they're expensive."

Sarah hesitated. She hadn't even bothered to think about the price. She knew Uncle Hyman couldn't afford to

spend too much. "Mr. Landau," she asked, "which are the cheapest?"

He pointed to a tray. "These — the plain gold with no chips."

The girls all looked at Uncle Hyman. Uncle Hyman looked at Mr. Landau. "And how much are the plain ones?"

"A dollar and some a little more — a dollar fifty, maybe."

"And this pair with the little blue stones?"

Sarah held her breath anxiously. Mr. Landau lifted the earrings out of the tray and examined them carefully. "Well now, I'll tell you, I know you're buying them for a present for Sarah. And Sarah's a good girl. So I'll make you a real bargain. I'll give you this pair for only two dollars."

"Two dollars!" the girls gasped.

She couldn't, Sarah decided unhappily, she just couldn't let him spend so much money. Uncle Hyman worked so hard. All day he tramped up and down the streets collecting old clothes. "No, Uncle Hyman," she said firmly, "I'll take the plain ones."

Uncle Hyman acted as if he hadn't heard her. He took out his purse, snapped open the clasp and poked around with his chubby fingers. "There seems to be enough here. Mr. Landau, we'll take the pair with the blue stones."

"Oh, Uncle Hyman! They're so beautiful, but you don't really have to. I'd be satisfied with just the plain ones, honest." Sarah's words tumbled over themselves, but her eyes sparkled as bright as the little blue stones.

Uncle Hyman shook his head. "No, never the plain ones. In Hebrew, Sarah means princess. And for a princess, you got to have nothing but the best." Carefully he counted out the money on Mr. Landau's showcase.

"Okay," said Mr. Landau. "Now we can get started."

He brought out a cigar box containing an assortment of items—a candle, a spool of white thread, matches, a package of large needles, and a bottle with a wick attached. It was filled with a colorless liquid. "Alcohol," Mr. Landau said. He touched a match to the wick. Instantly it flared up in a clear bluish flame. "Keep back, children," he warned. "Alcohol burns very hot!"

Then he cut off a piece of the white thread and ran it back and forth over the edge of the candle. "Why do you do that?" asked Sarah, her voice a bit quavery.

"I put a lot of wax on so the ears won't stick to it."

Sarah gave a shiver. Nervously she watched Mr. Landau thread a needle and hold it in the blue flame.

"That's to sterilize it," Ella explained.

"What's that?" Gertie wanted to know.

"Killing all the germs dead," Charlotte informed her.

"Oh," said Gertie, staring at the needle. Its point was already glowing red. "You mean there are bugs on the needle?"

"Not bugs — germs."

"But I don't see any!" Gertie insisted.

"I don't know. I guess they're all burned up already," Charlotte answered.

Now Mr. Landau was ready. "Come, Sarah," he said.

Sarah looked up at the jeweler with real fear in her eyes.

"Now, now." Mr. Landau patted her shoulder understandingly. "You don't have to be so frightened. It's a little nothing. I do it every single day of my life. To little girls, and to big girls, and to ladies, and I haven't killed anybody yet."

Sarah clenched her fists and held them tight against her sides. Mr. Landau said it was nothing. Anyhow, it'll only take a second.

Prick! Mr. Landau pushed the needle clear through Sarah's right earlobe, drawing the thread along with it. Then he cut the thread and tied it together forming a small loop. It was all done so quickly, Sarah didn't have time to let out more than a startled "ooh!" Bravely she stood quite still while the other ear was pierced.

"Sarah is sewed up!" Gertie squealed.

Another moment, and it was all over. Sarah had two loops of thread dangling on either side of her face. "It only hurt a teeny bit," she cried. "Mr. Landau, you're wonderful! You ought to be a doctor!"

The jeweler bowed. "Dr. Landau, that's me. Well, didn't I tell you it wouldn't hurt? That's because the ear is so soft. Now you must wear the thread for a couple of days. Then the holes will remain open and healed enough for me to put the earrings in."

With her arm in Uncle Hyman's, Sarah sailed out of Mr. Landau's store feeling like a real princess.

The next day when the children came home from school, Mama did not greet them with her usual cheerfulness. Nor did she ask how things had gone in school. There was a pensive look on her face as she went about serving them their afternoon snack. Only when they had finished eating did she speak. "Miss Carey came to see me today," she said. "She brought sad news. Guido's mother died yesterday. She was very, very ill," Mama went on gently. "Now she won't have to suffer anymore. She's at peace."

For a while no one could think of anything to say. Then Ella asked, "Mama, what will become of Guido?"

"Miss Carey expects him to live with her for the time

being. Meanwhile the settlement house will try to find out if there are any relatives. It's a pity on the child."

That night Sarah could not fall asleep. Inside her head, a host of sorrowful thoughts churned over and over. Guido has no Mama—no Papa, either. Just yesterday I was so happy. She put her hands up to her ears and felt the waxy cotton loops. While Uncle Hyman was buying me the earrings—Guido . . . Her eyes filled with tears. Oh, if only I could do something to make him less unhappy!

Then it came to her. She knew what she would do. She turned over and went fast asleep.

The following afternoon, a determined Sarah marched into the jewelry store. Mr. Landau came forward, smiling broadly. "So, you think it healed already? Well, let's take a look."

"No." Sarah spoke quickly. "Please, Mr. Landau—I don't want the earrings."

"You don't want them? You bought them already. You picked them out yourself, and your uncle paid me the money."

"I know, Mr. Landau. Only—" Sarah looked miserable. She kept twisting the corner of her sweater in her hand. It was hard to go on.

The jeweler frowned, puzzled. "What's the matter?

You don't like them, Sarah? You want maybe to change them for another pair?"

"Oh, no! I wouldn't want any other! These are just the most beautiful — and I love them! But you see, I have to give them up." She clasped her hands together tightly. "I need the money."

Mr. Landau gazed down at the earnest little face. "But why?"

So Sarah told him all about Guido. "Mr. Landau," she ended passionately, "it doesn't seem right that I should spend so much money on a pair of earrings. I have a mama, and a papa, and a lot of sisters, and even a brother. And Guido has nobody. I thought maybe a present would make him feel better. Then he'd know that at least he has friends."

Mr. Landau cocked his head thoughtfully. "Yes, little Sarah, that would be a very nice thing to do. Gladly I'll give you back the money. But what will your uncle say?"

"I asked him already."

"Then that's all right. So let me take out the thread. Then sometime when you get yourself another pair, you'll have the holes all ready." He snipped the loops and gently drew them out. Then he took some money from his cash drawer and counted it out into Sarah's palm.

"Thank you, Mr. Landau. Thank you an awful lot,"

Sarah cried, and sped homeward, the small fortune clutched tightly in her fist.

Henny was the first to notice the missing loops. "Sarah," she cried, "where are the earrings?"

Sarah spilled the money onto the kitchen table. "There they are," she said.

All eyes riveted on the money. "What's this?" Mama exclaimed.

"I took the money back for Guido," Sarah replied, haltingly. "He must be very unhappy — and I thought — I want to buy him a present. Please, Mama," she pleaded, "say it's all right."

Mama pulled the little girl close. "You are a good, generous child. Of course it's all right. What were you planning to get him for the money?"

"I don't know. I thought we could all talk it over."

"I've got some money saved up in my penny bank," Ella volunteered.

"I got a penny!" shouted Gertie. "Take my penny, Sarah!"

"I got three pennies!" Charlotte shouted even louder.

"Whyn't you tell me ahead of time," complained Henny. "Then maybe I could have had some money, too. Well, anyhow," she added brightly, "I'll help you pick out the present."

Ella counted up the donations. The total came to two dollars and twenty-one cents.

"Ma," asked Henny, "could you lend me four cents? Then it would be two twenty-five even. And you won't have to give me my after-lunch penny for four days."

"We could buy him a pair of shoes for that," Ella proposed.

Henny shook her head vigorously. "No, let's not buy him anything useful. Let's get him something for fun—like a baseball bat and a catcher's mitt."

"But he doesn't need them," Sarah objected. "They have lots of them at the settlement house and he always plays over there."

"How about roller skates?" suggested Charlotte.

"Why don't you let Sarah decide," Ella advised. "After all it was her idea. And it's mostly her money."

"That's right," the sisters assented. "You decide, Sarah."

So Sarah figured and figured. Finally she said, "Mama, how much does a very good shirt cost?"

"Maybe seventy-five cents."

"Could you get a pair of skates for one fifty?"

"Sure," interrupted Henny. "You could get a wonderful pair for that!"

"Then that's what we'll do," Sarah resolved. "Then he'll have something useful and something for fun."

It had taken several days of careful shopping, with Mama along to help. Ella had painted a beautiful design on a card with curlicues of flowers weaving all around. "For Guido" it said. Now the girls were on their way to Papa's shop to deliver the precious package.

"Guido will be 'sprised," Gertie said as she skipped along beside Charlotte.

"Uh huh," agreed Charlotte, squeezing Gertie's hand with excitement.

"I only hope he likes it," Sarah added.

Guido was in the back tying up bundles of old newspapers when they arrived. "Guido," Papa called, with a wink toward his daughters. "Some important people here to see you."

Guido came running and the girls immediately surrounded him. They noted how somber his face was and the deep shadows under his eyes. Sarah held out the package. "It's for you."

Gertie couldn't contain herself. "It's a present!"

"We all chipped in," Henny added.

"A present!" Guido repeated, blankly. "For me?" He scanned the circle of bright faces around him. "What you want to go spending money on me for?" he asked. His voice sounded gruff.

"Go on, Guido. Open the package," Papa prompted.

The girls stood on tiptoe with impatience. Would the wrapping never come off!

At long last, the gifts lay open to view. Guido stared at them, dumbfounded.

"Don't you like the present?" Sarah asked, alarmed. "The man in the store said he'll be glad to exchange them."

Guido fingered the smooth cotton material of the shirt. He picked up the skates. "Never had skates before." His face lit up. "I don't want to change anything. They're just great! Geewhiz, thanks!"

12: *Simchas Torah*

IT WAS THE MIDDLE of October and time for Jews everywhere to start building their little houses, succahs, in preparation for Succos, the week-long holiday of rejoicing and thanksgiving.

In Papa's backyard, work on the succah proceeded slowly. "You know, Mama," Papa remarked, "our girls are wonderful helpers. But what I need is someone for the heavier work."

"Why don't you have Guido come over and help you after school? You told me yourself he's very handy."

"Say, that's a good idea."

"By the way," Mama continued, "I took the baby to the clinic at the settlement house today. It was time for his regular check-up."

"So what happened?"

"Miss Carey says he's fine. He's just bursting with health. She also talked to me a little about Guido. She says Guido is studying very hard. He wants to make up the term he missed in school last year."

"That's good, Mama. There's nothing like keeping busy to help a person over a bad time."

"Still, Miss Carey says that sometimes at night she can hear him crying in his room."

"Naturally. He's still a child. He misses his mother."

So that very afternoon, Guido joined them at work in the yard. He seemed pleased to be with the family. Papa was glad he had gotten Guido to help. "He's strong, that boy, and such a worker!"

As the days followed one another the little succah began to take shape. Gradually Guido seemed to grow more lighthearted. Soon his boyish voice could be heard more and more frequently amidst the girl's chatter. At last there came a day when the sisters were delighted to hear him laugh out loud at one of Henny's antics.

The afternoon before Succos the succah was quite ready except for the decorations. But this was something that Guido did not want to be bothered with. He watched the girls busy themselves with scissors, colored paper, and

paste. "Making silly old paper chains and stuff!" he scoffed. "That's for sissies!"

Just then, Miss Carey walked in. "Could you use my help instead?" she asked with a smile.

"Hello, Miss Carey!" the children cried.

"So this is your succah. Guido raved so much about it, I just had to see it for myself." She went about examining and admiring everything—the strong, wooden walls, the homemade table and benches, and the pretty decorations. She sniffed with delight the scent of the fresh greenery festooning the walls and spread over the roof planks. "It's a child's perfect little dream house!" she exclaimed.

"Wait till it's really all fixed up, and Mama sets the table with a white tablecloth and the brass candlesticks!" Charlotte declared.

"Miss Carey," Mama asked, "would you and Guido like to join us tomorrow? We'd love to have you."

"Oh, thank you. It's so nice of you to ask us. Guido?"

Guido nodded his head in eager assent.

"Then we'll both see you in the succah."

"You know," Ella mused after they'd gone, "I've been thinking about Charlie and Kathy all day. I was wondering if they were remembering last year at this time."

She did not have to wonder for long. That afternoon's mail brought a letter from Chicago. "An anniversary note," Charlie and Kathy wrote, "for the happiest year of our lives brought about by our meeting in Papa's succah."

"It's certainly nice of them," Papa remarked. "You'd think being Gentiles and living so far away, they would have forgotten all about our holiday."

"Not those two," Mama said. "They wouldn't forget. After all, it was right here that they found each other again."

"It was just one year ago," reflected Sarah, "but it seems like ages."

"Ella," Mama said, "you write them back. Thank them for their letter and tell them we wish them many more such happy years to come."

Hardly was the letter sealed and stamped when Gertie stepped forward. "I want to put the letter in the letter box," she announced.

"Do you think you can reach it?" Papa asked with a broad smile.

"If I stand on tiptoe, I can."

"All right. Go ahead. But" – Papa held up a warning finger—"make sure to tell the little man inside the box where the letter is going, otherwise it'll never get there."

Gertie eyed Papa doubtfully. Surely, he must be joking. But there wasn't a trace of a smile on his face. Still, you never could tell with Papa. She opened the door and went out, wearing a somewhat baffled expression.

The sisters meanwhile had a hard time containing themselves.

"I think she really believed you, Papa," Charlotte howled.

166

Papa grinned. "Sure she did. The way you all believed it when you were little."

"Come on," suggested Henny. "Let's go after her and see what she does."

Still deliberating, Gertie was heading slowly toward the corner mail box, the letter clutched tightly in her hand. Should she do as Papa said? It seemed so silly. How could there be anybody in such a small box? Even if it was a midget. Well—what did it matter? It wouldn't hurt to holler out. Maybe that's what you're really supposed to do. Then, unaware that she was being watched by her sisters, she jiggled the slide and yelled into it. "Listen Mr. Man-in-the-box! This letter is going to Mr. and Mrs. Herbert Charles Graham in Chicago!"

For this Succos, Papa had bought a new luluv and esrog. The luluv is a tall palm branch to which are attached three myrtle twigs and two willow branches. The esrog is a citron, golden-yellow in color, spicy in aroma, and smooth to the touch.

"Papa," Gertie asked, "why do we need a luluv and esrog on Succos?"

Charlotte gave her a nudge. "Papa already explained it to you last year."

"I know. But I just can't remember."

"That's all right, Gertie," Papa told her. "The story can always bear repeating.

"In ancient times, when the Jews were farmers in the land of Palestine, they had fruitful harvests every year. But they never let themselves forget the hungry years when their forefathers had wandered in the desert before reaching the promised land. So in remembrance, they turned their fall harvest time, Succos, into a pilgrimage to the Holy City of Jerusalem. From every corner of the land the people came. They formed processions, carrying with them offerings of fruit and grain to lay before the Temple altar. As they went up to the Temple, they sang jubilantly and waved willow branches and palms. So to this day, even though Jews are scattered far and wide, they still celebrate the ceremony with the luluv and esrog as a reminder of those early times.

"And now, let us begin our ceremony," Papa finished. "Ella, you first."

Whereupon Papa placed the luluv in Ella's right hand and the esrog in her left. He pronounced a prayer of blessing in Hebrew. Ella repeated the words after him, and shook the luluv lightly in all directions—north, south, east, and west, as well as up, down, forward, and back, in affirmation that the Lord is everywhere and the earth is full of His bounty.

Each child in turn performed the same ceremony, which would be repeated every morning for the first seven mornings of the festival.

On the first two days, Papa did not work, and the children stayed home from school. The family went to synagogue. The luluv and esrog went too, proudly borne by Papa. All three, Papa, luluv and esrog, played their part in the ancient ritual in the synagogue.

The in-between days of the festival were uneventful. The children were back at school and were it not for the morning ceremony in the succah, it might have seemed like any other week. On the morning of the seventh day, the luluv was shaken and the esrog taken up for the last time. For the last time also, the evening meal was eaten in the Succah. But the holiday was not yet over.

Evening of the eighth day found Gertie dancing around Mama as she was laying out their holiday clothes. "We're getting all dressed up!" she crowed happily.

"Of course," Mama said. "I want my girls to look their nicest at the synagogue."

"Papa"– Charlotte's face screwed up quizzically–"it's Simchas Torah now, isn't it?"

"Yes."

"And Simchas Torah means joy in the Torah, doesn't it?"

"Yes."

"So what has that got to do with a harvest festival?"

Papa nodded. "That's a good question, Charlotte, and it deserves a good answer. You see, after the days of rejoicing in the harvest, the Jews added a couple more days for rejoicing in the Torah. As you know, our Torah tells of the history of our people as well as its laws. All throughout the year, portions of the Torah are read during services. On Simchas Torah we come to the end of the reading and right away, we start all over again with the very first chapter – Genesis. We Jews have always been happy with our Torah, and that is why Simchas Torah is such a jolly time."

"Come now, girls, hurry up and get dressed," Mama cautioned. "We musn't be late."

Quickly the girls put on their holiday clothes. Afterward, Mama examined them critically – from the top of their heads, where the ribbon bows stood up like butterfly wings, to their black patent leather shoes. "Yes," she murmured approvingly, "you all look lovely."

"Rubbing butter on our shoes was a marvelous idea," Charlotte whispered. "Look, Gertie, how shiny they look."

"And they squeak!" Gertie added. "They'll all know we've got new shoes!"

Down the stairs and into the street trooped the family with Papa and baby Charlie heading the parade. Other Papas and Mamas were also walking with their children, all dressed in their best. The very air crackled with holiday spirit. Grown-ups greeted one another and the youngsters laughed and carried on all the way.

At the synagogue, Papa and the younger children threaded their way through the crowd to find seats together on the hard wooden benches. Mama, holding Charlie in her arms, and Ella joined the women in the rear.

The congregation quieted down, and the evening service was chanted.

Gertie poked Sarah. "When are we going to march?"

"Shush. There goes the rabbi now."

Gertie watched with awe as the Torah Scrolls were taken out of the ark. First the rabbi, then several men of the congregation, each holding a Torah in his arms, proceeded up the aisle, singing as they went. Reverently the sisters pressed forward with the other worshippers to kiss the scrolls. Then they joined the line of marchers behind the bearers of the Holy Books. Around about the synagogue and up to the platform moved the procession. Then the precious scrolls

were handed over to other waiting arms. Round and round they marched, young and old — seven times around, singing joyously.

From the back of the synagogue, Uncle Solomon's voice suddenly rang out:

"All the world is dancing, singing
on this joyous holiday!"

Right hand cupping his right ear, left arm flung wide, he began shuffling his feet in time with his song.

The sisters stared at him, astonished. Could this be their dignified Uncle Solomon?

"Papa, he's dancing!" Gertie shouted. "Is it a party?"

"Yes, my little one," Papa cried gaily. "It's God's party and everyone is invited!"

Uncle Solomon's feet kept whirling faster and faster. They were carrying him clear across the back of the synagogue. He did not dance alone for long. One after another joined in to form a circle. Pious old men forgot the stiffness in their aching joints and danced shoulder to shoulder with the younger men and children. The curtain separating men and women was thrust aside, and so contagious was the revelry, many of the younger women joined the dancers.

In and out and roundabout, Uncle Solomon led them, and the excitement kept mounting. Voices feebly raised at first, soared ecstatically higher. Feet that had moved hesitantly, quickened their pace. Only the older women remained seated on the benches, bobbing their heads and clapping their work-worn hands in time with the dancers. Mama, too, was caught up in the merriment, bouncing a delighted Charlie up and down on her knee.

The sisters, swept along in the general furor, were prancing about in all directions. Tiny Gertie was hemmed in by a sea of moving legs till Papa swung her onto his shoulders. There she rode on her bobbing throne, smiling down triumphantly at Charlotte who was holding on for dear life to her dancing Papa.

Such hilarious goings on could not last forever. Even as

they had joined, so now the dancers fell out as one by one they grew exhausted. In the end, only Uncle Solomon danced on, until at last he, too, had no more strength to continue. But the exultant singing persisted even after the Torah Scrolls had been set back into the ark.

Now sweet wine and cakes were served to the grownups, and for the youngsters there were cookies, nuts, and fruit.

The joyous expression of their love for the Torah once again had brought this small community close together. A feeling of harmony and good cheer pervaded all as they stood about munching and exchanging pleasantries. Jews everywhere would go on as one, with renewed strength to face the year ahead.

After Simchas Torah, the little house in the backyard belonged solely to the children to use as they pleased. When some weeks later, Papa announced that it would have to come down, they were not too unhappy. What Ella said was only too true—"We'll build a much better one next year."

13: *A Thanksgiving To Remember*

THANKSGIVING was a joyful day for the youngsters on the East Side. Most of them, trailing the oversized clothing of their Mamas and Papas, scooted up and down the narrow streets. Faces streaked with red and black smudges, they besieged the passersby, clamoring loudly, "Anything for Thanksgiving?" Those who turned them down risked being swatted with a stocking filled with flour.

Today there was to be a Thanksgiving party at the settlement house and Mama's girls were invited.

"We're lucky!" Charlotte cried. "We've got two Thanksgivings to celebrate — Succos and then our country's."

There was a knock on the door and in came Tanta.

"Oh, my, look at you!" she exclaimed. "All dressed up. What's happening?"

"A party!" yelled Gertie. "At the settlement house!"

"They look nice, don't they?" Mama declared proudly.

"And why shouldn't they?" replied Tanta. "They're beautiful girls, all of my nieces."

"Tanta, will you be here when we get back?" Ella asked.

"Of course she will," Mama answered for Tanta. "She's staying for supper."

"I am? That's nice." Tanta followed the children to the door. "Mind you take care how you cross the street and watch out for the trolley."

"I think I'll go back to the shop for awhile," observed Papa. "I have some work to finish up."

"All right, Papa, but come home early. After all, it's a holiday."

Mama picked up her knitting and settled herself in the comfortable rocker. She gave a sigh of contentment. "It's so quiet and peaceful now."

The time slipped pleasantly by while Mama rocked and knitted and listened to Tanta's cheerful gossip. "You know," Mama said after awhile, "I haven't seen cousin Leah for such a long time. She can't walk so far and it's not so easy for me to get away, what with the children and everything. She wants especially to see the baby so much. I wish I could go over."

"Well, why don't you go right now? Is it supper you're concerned about? I can take care of it."

"You're so kind. We had a big dinner anyway, and the

children will probaby be eating a lot of sweets at the party. I think some rice and milk would be good. They like it, especially with cinnamon. You'll find just enough rice in the cereal set and . . . ."

"That's all you're going to serve for supper?"

"Don't worry. There's plenty more things in the ice-box."

"So go already," Tanta urged. "I know where everything is."

While Mama redressed, Tanta prettied up the baby. "Thank you a lot," Mama said. "I'll try not to stay too long."

"Take your time," Tanta called after her. "A chance like this you don't get so often."

As the door closed, Tanta put on Mama's apron and set to work. She measured out the milk and added the rice and seasoning. When the milk had come to a boil, she pushed the pot toward the back of the stove to simmer and sat down in Mama's rocking chair. It's so comfortable here, she thought. It's good to have a day off from work. The rocker went slower and slower; her head drooped, and soon she was asleep.

The minutes ticked by. Tanta was dreaming of the days when she was a young girl in the old country. A beau came courting in a carriage drawn by two magnificent horses. The whole town was standing on the rooftops to witness the sight! She could hear the hoofbeats as they went clippety clop on the dirt road. Clippety clop—clippety clop! They were coming nearer! She woke with a start!

It was the children bounding up the stairs and into the kitchen, their faces rosy with the cold and excitement. Close behind them came Miss Carey and Guido.

"Gosh, what's that awful smell?" Ella shouted.

"Something's burning!" exclaimed Miss Carey.

"My rice and milk!" wailed Tanta as she sprang toward the stove. Hurriedly she grabbed a dishrag, lifted the blackened pot, and dropped it into the sink. "This was supposed to be your supper," she remarked ruefully as she turned on the faucet. The cold water hissed and steamed against the sides of the pot.

"Open the window!" yelled Henny. "And the door!" She sprinted about the kitchen obeying her own commands.

"Everything happens to me!" Tanta moaned in distress. "Now what'll I do?" She scrubbed away frantically at the bespattered stove. "And soon Mama will be here!" A deep frown furrowed her brow. She was thinking hard. Then her face brightened. "I know! I'll make a false soup. That won't take long."

"A false soup? What kind of soup is that?" asked Miss Carey.

"When you haven't got any meat or bones and such, you use other things to give it a taste."

"What kind of things?" Miss Carey prompted.

Tanta threw up her hands. "I don't have time to explain. If you'll watch, you'll see." She fairly flew to the icebox and the cupboard, taking out all sorts of odds and ends. "Better yet," her voice rose shrilly, "if you'll all help, maybe we'll get it done before Mama comes."

"Yes, yes! What shall we do?" the girls cried.

Miss Carey laughed. "I'll scrub out the pot so Mama'll never know."

"No, let me do it!" cried Guido, rolling up his sleeves.

Everyone rushed around here and there. Tanta put Ella to work frying onions while the others washed and diced carrots, celery, cabbage, tomato, a white turnip, a parsnip and several big potatoes. In the meantime, Tanta had melted a large dab of butter in a soup pot. Adding some flour, she stirred the mixture till it was browned smooth and free of lumps. Into the soup pot went the onions, seasoning, and all the rest of the vegetables and water.

Tanta began hunting through the kitchen cabinet.

"What are you looking for now?" asked Ella.

"To see if Mama has any farfel. (Noodle dough chopped into small bits.) It would be just the right thing to finish off with." She peered into a paper bag. "Ah! Here's some!" Quickly she measured out a cupful.

In a little while, the soup was bubbling. Soon its savory odor drove away the unpleasant smell of the scorched rice and milk. The telltale pot was already shining brightly on the shelf. At last, Tanta could breathe more easily. "Please, everyone," she implored, "remember now! Not a word to Mama, or I'll never hear the end of this."

Everyone laughingly promised. Not a minute too soon, for the door swung open and in walked Mama. Henny took the baby from her and started removing his sweater and leggings.

"Oh, Miss Carey is here! Guido, too," Mama said, pleased. "Thank you for walking the children home."

"Not at all," replied Miss Carey. "We wanted to come."

Gertie tugged at Mama's sleeve. "Miss Carey got all dressed up for the party, too."

"Yes," said Mama, looking with admiration at Miss Carey's dress. "Maroon satin! It's very becoming!"

"You look sort of unfamiliar without your uniform on," remarked Ella.

"Yes, but she looks lovely," Charlotte added.

"She sure does!" Gertie chimed in.

"Thank you," replied Miss Carey. "I'm glad you're all agreed." There was a merry tinkle in her voice. She seemed carefree and lighthearted.

"Well, children, how was the party?" Mama asked.

Everybody wanted to talk first. "You should have seen it!" Sarah cried. "The place was all decorated with streamers and lanterns. And there were pumpkins and dried ears of corn — you know — the red kind all strung up, and tacked up on the walls were pictures of turkeys and pilgrims and —"

"Mama, they had flowers." Charlotte could not contain herself. "Can you imagine! Real, live flowers! They were beautiful! In vases with leaves all colors, yellow and red and brown."

"But what I liked the best was the punch and ice cream. With cookies!" added Gertie.

"And you know what, Ma?" gushed Henny. "There was a dopey boy following Ella around the place. He was making goo-goo eyes at her the whole time. And Ma . . ."

"Keep still!" Ella stopped her. Quickly she changed the conversation. "The nicest thing of all was the play."

"They all spoke with thees and thous," Sarah took up

the tale. "Afterward everybody in the audience went around talking that way. It sounded so funny we couldn't stop laughing."

"Guido was in the play," said Charlotte.

Henny ran over to Guido. "Thou gavest a fine performance," she said, bowing low. "We all thank thee."

"Aw g'wan!" Guido said, joining in the merriment.

"It certainly sounds like you all had a good time," declared Mama. "Miss Carey, there isn't much for supper, but we must have you and Guido stay and share it with us."

"Thank you very much," Miss Carey answered. "I'd like especially to sample Tanta's cooking," she added with a wink at Tanta.

When Papa returned from the shop, he put an extra leaf in the kitchen table to make room for all. Tanta insisted she'd do the serving. "Tonight you'll be a lady," she told Mama. She set the steaming bowls of soup on the table. Mama eyed her bowl wonderingly. "This is rice and milk?" she asked.

The conspirators exchanged knowing glances.

"Rice and milk she wants," Tanta announced to no one in particular. "Without a drop of rice left in the whole house."

Eyebrows arched, Mama said, "I could have sworn there was some." She took a taste and smiled up at Tanta. "What you made is even better. Delicious!"

Everyone except Papa began to titter. Mama looked around her, puzzled. "Did I say something funny?"

Miss Carey came to the rescue. "It's just that everyone feels so happy today." She paused a moment. "Especially Guido and I. We have something extra to be thankful for." Guido's hand and hers intertwined. "We wanted you to be the first to know."

Everyone fell silent. Papa's spoon stopped in midair.

Miss Carey went on. "Guido's going to live with me for good."

Gertie peered through her fingers at Miss Carey. "You mean Guido is like a son and you will be his new mama?"

"Mama!"

Everyone turned in astonishment. It was baby Charlie! He was standing up in his high chair, waving his spoon, looking very pleased with himself.

"It talks!" screeched Charlotte. And the room rocked with laughter.

Charlie gurgled. He knew he had done something smart.

Papa looked around at the happy faces. "This is surely a Thanksgiving to remember." He rapped his spoon on the table. "Tanta!" he shouted. "I'll have another bowl of your wonderful soup!"